[A]n absolutely brilliant debut novella....Asad introduces each of the gods and goddesses in a fresh way while maintaining the traditional traits of each one. The world is vivid, emotions run high, and real-life challenges are met head-on.

— REEDSY DISCOVERY

Asad's writing is vivid and descriptive—making it impossible not to feel as if you have climbed through a vibrantly drawn storybook, or crept right into the scene in the middle of a cinematic otherworldly battle.

— INDEPENDENT BOOK REVIEW

[Rizwan Asad] majestically resurrects the gods to human form....Superb!

— READERS' FAVORITE

Rizwan Asad has crafted a fun, thrilling take on contemporary mythology—now we know what the Greek gods and goddesses have been up to all this time!

> — DAVE PASQUANTONIO, AUTHOR OF "THE MATILDAS"

A well written, funny, and engaging book about what happens to the Greek Gods who survived to the modern age.

> — STEVE RODGERS, AUTHOR OF "CITY OF SHARDS"

DIO IN THE DARK

DIO IN THE DARK

RIZWAN ASAD

Ness House Press

Dio in the Dark by Rizwan Asad

Published by Ness House Press

Copyright © 2021 Rizwan Asad

All rights reserved.

No part of this book may be reproduced in any form or by any electronic or mechanical means, including information storage and retrieval systems, without written permission from the author, except for the use of brief quotations in a book review.

This is a work of fiction. Names, characters, places, and incidents are products of the author's imagination or are used fictitiously. Any resemblance to actual persons, living or dead, businesses, companies, events, or locales is entirely coincidental.

Cover Design & Illustration by Casey Gerber.

ISBN: 978-1-7778757-0-1

CHAPTER 1

Steel crashed against steel and reverberated between the buildings and down the pre-dawn street. The mechanical steed tossed back and swallowed the contents of a dumpster before lurching and heaving the box back onto the pavement.

"Excellent!" said Zeus. "My pet feeds well today!"

Zeus, god of thunder, overseer of the universe, the lightning hurling King of the Gods himself, sprang easily to grab the handle and land on the running board of the garbage truck. He wore dirty blue overalls and work boots. The back of his overalls read, "Barker Sanitation," and the front, over his immortal heart, had a patch that said "Zed."

Zed didn't command the type of respect afforded to ZEUS: KING OF THE GODS, but it raised fewer questions and eyebrows. Zed had an easier time dealing with the mailman or signing up for a mobile phone contract. Zed blended in; Zeus stuck out like a volcano.

Sacrifices had been made in the name of subtlety. Zeus, for example, had set aside more than his name. While Zeus was a proud and powerful deity, Zed was a humble sanitation worker with little say in the workings of the world around him. He had even shaved his epic beard so that he might lay a little lower. Where there was once a thick and majestic mane impervious to all harm, he now wore a slight, ill-conceived goatee, greying unevenly on the left side.

"Yo, Zed!" called a voice from within the rumbling diesel truck. It was Jack, the truck's driver, and Zeus' early-morning colleague. "It's quittin' time, Big Poppa."

Zeus (which we may as well call him here, for what is a god without his immortal moniker?) had worked hard to blend in, but there were some aspects of his demeanor and personality that could not go unnoticed. It was not just his massive bulk and peculiar accent, but his pride and virility that made him conspicuous. One might be able to miss the six-foot-seven hulk in the room, until he gets a little too inebriated and yanks a stubborn door off its hinges, a scenario Zeus had found himself in far too often.

"Yes," he replied. "It is indeed time to give our earthly bodies some much needed rest." He spoke with easy gravity, in the manner of a man who has some deep understanding of eternity. "The day is at hand and soon my city will awaken—"

"Cool, Big Poppa," came the unenthusiastic reply from the cab of the truck.

"—and night will fall. The Darkness will return. Have I told you about The Darkness, young one?"

"I know, I know," replied the driver. "You tell me about The Darkness every freakin' Friday. And this 'young one' business? Man, I'm sixty-two years old! Only thing young about me is my teeth, and even them is gettin' to be teenagers!"

"The Darkness," Zeus went on, undeterred. "Not merely the absence of light, but a wicked foe, an evil, visceral being from beyond the realm of time..."

"Please, Zed. You gotta knock that noise off man. I'm tired and I wanna go home..." The driver paused, thinking, then continued in a sly tone. "You should hurry along, too, y'know, what with The Darkness coming and all."

Yet, while the old man joked and chided, there was truth in his warning. There was a Darkness that was so much more than the absence of light. It was an evil untold, and Zeus had felt it growing, coming in like the tide, in a way he had not felt in millennia. Each evening, with the dying of the sun, the cold presence of The Darkness cascaded through the city in waves. Mortals were unaware of this presence, but Zeus was not fooled, he knew this Darkness was not merely night.

For nine months, he had experienced a growing and unsettling presence in the hours between dusk and dawn. It was something substantial, tangible. It enveloped him like a snake devouring its prey and played about the edges of his consciousness like a waking dream. It watched him from the blackest shadows, hooded eyes calculating, measuring, waiting. He knew it had a name, and he sensed that he had once spoken that cursed word, though it was lost to him now. He was too proud to admit it, but he was afraid. He knew that this Darkness, whatever it was, would consume him.

※

THERE WAS A TIME, ABOUT SIX HUNDRED YEARS AGO, when Zeus had taken it upon himself to be protector of the mortals. It was a short-lived experiment, in part due to the costume he had chosen: the black armor of a knight fallen from grace, a long, red feather emerging jauntily from the crest of the helmet. But medieval armor is cumbersome. Wear it while wielding bolts of lightning, and you have a potentially deadly scenario.

Another reason he had eventually slipped out of a protector role and away from mortal memory was because there was simply no worthy villain to protect the mortals from. They were, themselves, their greatest enemy, and there was nothing Zeus could do to rescue them from their own greed and hatred. Besides, his wife, Hera, had teased him mercilessly about the costume.

More recently, Zeus gave the protector role another

go, but he found himself often confused with a Norse god, much to his embarrassment. He may have been a lot of things, but he was certainly not one of those savages. What was worse than being confused for the Norse was being tabbed as an "old cosplay dude," as he had been called last year by a slovenly youth with a ring through his lip.

He had previously tried the route of understatement. Dark jeans, green plaid shirt, a red ball cap to echo the red cloak of his past adventures. But this ensemble proved to be underwhelming, not heroic. His appearance did not inspire hope or awe or adventure. He blended in when he was not trying to, curiously enough, and the look was less conspicuous than what he had now adopted as his everyday outfit: ripped, acid-washed jeans, a white T-shirt that stretched so tightly across his massive chest and shoulders that it strained at the seams, and the same red ball cap, which he usually carried in his back pocket.

That cap held special significance for Zeus. He had won it at a mortal carnival, calling upon the last of his godly magic in summoning a gust of wind to knock down a stack of battered bowling pins. He had been trying to impress a young woman named Brooke. She was unmoved and he never saw her again, but he kept the cap anyway— Bruce Springsteen had one just like it. If it was good enough for The Boss, it was good enough for the King of the Gods.

The house at 12 Mountain View was towering and imposing, yet somehow impressive in its elegant decrepitude. Out front there was a dry pond bed, the shattered remains of a broken, fluted pillar, and a charred fence. The cracked, stained-glass windows glowed yellow, orange, and red, and in the evenings cast an amber glow onto the front lawn, dimly illuminating the wreckage of a chariot in a strange, dystopian tableaux.

It may have looked like an ancient junkyard or a neglected museum of antiquities, but to the residents of 12 Mountain View, this house represented a timeless romanticism. The house was, in itself, a story. It was a story told time and time again in the incoherent and nostalgia-filled ramblings of a man who was never fully aware that he had told it before. The home portrayed eons of history in a single glance. It was a good and solid home in many ways, and it was not easily viewed from any main thoroughfare. Indeed, it was a difficult place to reach, at least, for any mortal soul.

Dio was staring out the window of his attic bedroom when his father returned.

Ugh, he thought.

A door slammed somewhere downstairs.

King of the Gods. Murderer of mothers. Father of the year... Oh, wait...a bunch of years. Totally.

"Dio? Are you up here?"

Zeus' voice boomed through the dimly lit attic as he stuck his head up through a door in the floor that was far too narrow for his massive shoulders.

Of course I am, o' Usurper of Happiness. Where else would I be? Afflicted with this curse of unending mortality...

"Dionysus?"

"I told you never to call me that!" Dio shouted, leaping to his feet and emerging from his bed near the window. He wore a silk kimono, printed all over with delicate, red flowers. His cheeks were stubbled, and his eyes were dark with traces of old eyeliner.

"Why not?" replied the King of the Gods, jovially, his somewhat Greek/somewhat everywhere accent thicker than before. "Dionysus is a lovely name!"

"Dionysus is dead! Just like my mother, who you killed!"

"My child..." said Zeus, his voice sounding suddenly weary and grieved. He had treaded the waters of this conversation with his son many, many times before.

"I am not your son! I am Dio, the twice born! And I will have my revenge!" Dio had lost control of his pitch during the outburst, and what began as an anguished cry had morphed into a high-pitched shriek by the end of the sentence. Aware of how he sounded, Dio fell silent, his mouth working as though to form words, but no more sound coming forth.

"Semele...your mother...she was such a beautiful woman," Zeus said, his words full of tenderness and sorrow. "She was the unfortunate victim of a cruel and heinous act. But in her ashes, I found you."

The atmosphere in the room was heavy, as though the space between the bare rafters was filled with its own, colorless gravity.

"I carried you, as you know...just as though you were in your mother's womb. I sewed you into my own thigh and I waited for you to be ready for—"

"But you killed her," Dio interrupted.

There was a long and loaded silence in which the hearts of both men broke, as they had broken time and time again over the centuries.

"I did," said Zeus.

※

Several hours after Zeus had left the attic, Dio slipped out of his room and made his way across the top floor of the house to the spiral staircase in the back. He descended the steel steps, his shoes clattering on the iron, and walked through the backyard to the small greenhouse.

It was the place he always went when he and his father fought about Semele and her fate, which was often.

Inside, the greenhouse was hot and quiet and pleasant. He would move amongst the orchids and the roses, the exotic and the simple and the impossible plants that he grew and kept here.

The thorn of a rose snagged the sleeve of his kimono. Dio plucked the offending bud and dropped it into a glass. From a drawer below a worktable he pulled an unlabeled bottle half full of a clear spirit. Dio added the liquor to the glass with the rose and sat on a high stool to sip his drink. He caught his own reflection in the greenhouse glass and brushed a lock of dark, disheveled hair away from his face.

It had been thousands of years since his mother's death, but it was only in the last twenty or so that he had begun to feel the pain of her absence so acutely. It could have been his waning powers or a slowly developing aspect of maturity, but he was beginning to feel as though he were filling up with pain and angst and anger and would soon reach full capacity, and he did not know what would occur once that happened. Perhaps the god of wine and ritual madness was really no more than a divine son unable to cope with the loss of his mortal mother.

And perhaps it was none of those things. Though causation unknown, only one thing could be certain: everything was a mess.

Maybe, just maybe, tonight could change that. It was a thought Dio had most every night, no matter how many times it proved to be wrong. It was with some perverse sense of hope that he ventured out into the night and into the company of mortals, time and time again. He would go out into the artificially lit city, and his memories would become a blur of darkly lit corners, faceless women in designer dresses, and with any luck, the fleeting pleasure of feeling absolutely nothing.

Dio tossed back the last of his drink and left the glass, with the soaked and curling rose bud, beside the bottle on the table. Then he turned out the lights on his way back to his room to get dressed for the evening.

※

"HE NEVER CLOSES THE DOOR," COMPLAINED APOLLO, who, as fate would have it, had been able to retain his true name in the time of mortals. There were enough humans named Apollo—whether they were named after the god or the movie boxer, no one could be sure— that the name had become a passable moniker for blending into the world.

Apollo watched Dio's silhouette dissolve into the darkness as he walked off the house's grounds. Despite the days of sulking and sleeping, and the nights of drink and debauchery, Dio still had the same figure as always: tall and lean, with muscular, rounded shoulders.

"I mean, I get it, he's a brooding playboy with a heart of gold, or whatever, but c'mon, he can at least button up his shirt! It's October and we aren't in Greece anymore. We're not trying to heat the whole neighborhood!"

Zeus, preoccupied with trying on his latest "protector of the mortals" garb, did not reply. He stood before a full-length mirror and frowned at his own reflection, trying to fathom why tights were all the rage when it came to dressing like a hero in the modern age.

Apollo sat down heavily on a lavish and overstuffed sofa in the large living room and picked up his guitar.

"Hello, Ebony," he said softly, as he strummed lightly on the black Fender Stratocaster. The electric guitar was not plugged into an amplifier, but in Apollo's divinely talented hands, it did not need to be. The melody that he picked and strummed resonated through the room with a clarity and delicacy that defied reason. His nimble fingers sought the melody as fish find their way through a stream—without effort—and even Zeus paused and turned an ear to listen, with peace and delight on his features.

"You are still a god among us," Zeus said.

Apollo did not stop playing as he replied, "There is magic in music, a kind that does not expire with the passing of time or the waning of worshipers."

He paused, sighing with a sadness Zeus had not witnessed in many years, before fishing a cigarette out from the pocket of his wrinkled linen shirt.

"When are you going to give up on this whole superhero business, Dad?"

Zeus turned to face his son directly and looked at him with earnest eyes.

"You have felt it, Apollo. You know something this way comes."

Apollo set his Strat aside, leaned forward, and tapped the ash from his cigarette into a cut glass tray on the mahogany coffee table.

"Alright, let's say that there is something wrong, something vile moving out there in the darkness." Apollo waved his arms around his head, seeming to gesture at the world unseen while simultaneously trying to conjure a spell that might convince his father to drop his nonsensical fears. "Let's say that The Darkness really is some sort of evil that has somehow survived eons without any of us discovering it. Do you really expect to scare it away by dressing up in lime-green tights?"

Zeus turned to observe himself in the mirror again. "No, I suppose not. But what am I supposed to do? Those copycats at Marvel have taken all the good costume ideas! Did I tell you about the time someone got me confused with Tho—"

"Hold on," Apollo interrupted. He took one last quick drag from his smoke, crushed it out in the ashtray, and rose from his seat. "Gotta go."

And just like that, he was gone. Yet, Zeus was not alone in the room.

"Hello, sweet brother," the god of the underworld spoke, his voice seeming to slither with elongated E's and S's that almost hissed. He appeared with a smile on his face so wide that it was as though a crescent moon had found its home in his mouth.

"Hello, Hades," Zeus said as he wondered how Apollo always managed to leave just in time to avoid having to speak to his uncle. "How's the insurance business going?"

"Oh, very lucrative."

Hades was dressed from head to toe in black. But not just black—Armani black. Haute couture black. The deep blue-black of success. The kind of black that comes with a tailor and one hell of a price tag.

"You know what I always say," Hades said. "Insurance is like a parachute: if it isn't there the first time, it's not likely you'll be needing it again."

The lord of the dead grinned in a way that made Zeus think of a shark closing in on an unsuspecting swimmer.

"And of course...I get their souls, too."

As he spoke, Hades conjured an orb atop his open palm, glowing a dark and putrid green. His smile grew ever wider.

"Mind boggling, isn't it, brother?"

Zeus raised his eyebrows. "What?"

"The world has forgotten you and left you powerless, yet they still fret and worry about a power like mine."

Zeus grunted and turned back to the mirror once more. "You are not as powerful as you once were, Hades."

Hades ran his long, pale fingers through his slicked back hair as Zeus went on.

"Aphrodite can still smite you, with barely even the force of her delicate little finger."

What Zeus said was true. Despite all the other gods having been forgotten millennia before, Aphrodite had continued to be worshiped through the ages. And there was never a time more fitting for a goddess like Aphrodite than the present, the era of social media, where a single selfie could garner legions of followers. Indeed, the cult of Aphrodite had never been so strong.

"Perhaps that is true," Hades conceded. "It is a shame that she is too busy staring at her own reflection to concern herself with what is upon us now."

"So you have felt The Darkness as well." Zeus' tone was serious. Finally, someone else acknowledged that something was amiss. "What do you know of it?"

Hades raised a finger and waved it playfully in Zeus' face.

"Nuh-uh-uh," he chided. "Never without a deal first."

"And what do you want?"

Hades' smile turned malevolent, and his eyes narrowed to slits. "Oh, sweet brother, what I want, I've already got."

The landline rang. Zeus moved to answer but Hades made a quick gesture with his hand and Zeus found himself unable to move. In short time, the answering machine picked up.

A shaky and familiar voice came through the speaker.

"Um...hello. H-hello? I'm looking for Big Pop—. Is this thing working? I'm looking for Zed. This is Jack from Barker Sanitation and he's not been to work in a week. I'm kinda worried about him, ya know? Anyway, I went to the home address he had listed...12 Mountain View...but it was just an old, abandoned building... umm...well..." There was a click, and the machine went silent.

"Hades...what have you done?"

CHAPTER 2

T he air was heavy and hot, filled with the smells of sweat and liquor, of red wine and heavy breath. Of lust.

With his eyes closed and his head tilted back, Dio could imagine himself at one of his glorious festivals, the heedless bacchanals of the old times, in the old country. The air was the same, as were the sensations. Hands all over his body, desirous fingers pressing into his flesh and playing with his sweat-soaked hair. He felt the bodies of men and women alike gravitate around him as though he were the sun, the center of the known universe, and they were merely adoring planets, obediently orbiting in the dark.

The music was different now. The throbbing bass of the club was a far cry from the drums and flutes of those ancient mountain retreats. He could feel the rhythm pulsing through the dance floor, up through his feet, and into his joints and marrow, filling him, and most importantly, blocking out the bleating and pleading voices of his devotees.

Yes, this was much preferable to dancing around a bonfire and sleeping on the ground. There was indoor plumbing, a well-stocked bar, a gyro shop right around the corner that stayed open until 3 a.m. on weekends. Yet, this modern debauchery was lacking something of the old world: belief.

Whereas once Dio had led a band of loyal and obsessive adherents, he now only commanded the attentions of these club rats and burnouts that fell under his power in a time and place where they would have most likely been drunk anyway. There was no faith or loyalty; this partying was entirely unprincipled. Night after night, Dio hit the clubs and waded into the sea of twenty-somethings, like a magnet attracting those with the biggest and emptiest voids, drawing them to him only to toss them away when the lights came back on and the DJ announced: "You don't have to go home, but you can't stay here."

And when that happened, he could always find a club that stayed open later, or a house party or rave. Somewhere in the ever-deepening Toronto night, there was always a party going on, and Dio didn't need an app or an invite to find it. His blood pulled him, tide-like, to wherever the "good times" were going on. He was power in a vacuum.

And, more and more, he saw little point in going home anyway.

His father had been missing for months. Without Zeus—void of magic as he was—to act as a point of centrality, the other gods no longer found reason to visit the home on Mountain View, or its residents. Indeed, without the will of Zeus to anchor the Olympians to the city, many of the other gods seemed to orbit farther and farther away. Cupid was the first to leave the city—without so much as a goodbye, he simply vanished. Aphrodite's departure came with several announcements, each one thanking the city of Toronto and welcoming herself to her new home in Los Angeles.

Apollo had become despondent and moped around the house all day and night, plucking out increasingly angsty tunes on his ever-present Strat, drinking craft beer by the barrel, and kicking over furniture. Dio's brother had taken a distressing turn and would talk to the walls until the sun came up in the morning and he finally passed out on the couch, where Dio would find him when he eventually wandered home.

Nobody knew where Zeus had gone, but that didn't mean that no one was looking. Poseidon had ordered the docks and inlets dragged. Not that Zeus could drown, but there was little more that old Uncle P could do. He himself was so addled with rum that he rarely ever left his houseboat. His argument had been that the sea holds all secrets, so something on that muddy bottom must point to where Zeus had gone. All he had turned up were some old anchors, a couple of tires, and a whole lot of plastic water bottles.

Aunt Ino—the once-mortal sister of Dio's own mortal mother—had also been in touch, in her own eccentric way: notes scrawled on discarded newspapers and left on the front porch of the house at 12 Mountain View said that she was "keeping her ear to the ground" and was asking amongst her circles if anyone had word on Zed the garbage man. Though she had raised him as a child, Dio had his doubts about the one-time queen's current circle of acquaintances. He was certain, however, that she kept an ear to the ground, or at least a park bench.

Even Aphrodite had devoted one entire tweet to seeking out information that might lead to the whereabouts of her old friend. She had included a photo of herself and Zeus, carefully photoshopped to remove the pristine pillars of the Acropolis—brand new at the time — in the background. All it managed to accomplish was trimming her legion of followers—it seemed, anytime her messaging turned away from her own brand of beauty and happiness, her worshipers turned to someone else.

It appeared that no one knew what had become of Dio's father—and very few people cared. He was, after all, just a sanitation worker. People went missing every day in Toronto. Sometimes they turned up in a flophouse or in jail or floating in the Don River. Sometimes they didn't turn up at all.

Athena had placed an anonymous call to the police, but once the cops realized that it was Zed the wannabe superhero they were looking into, they quickly shrugged it off, assuming he was off doing something ridiculous.

"Did you check his fortress of solitude?" one officer had mockingly inquired.

This had become the new normal. Zeus was gone, and Dio could not decide whether to care or not. He had cursed his father's name for centuries, wished the most horrible of fates upon him, and now he was gone. He knew he should be jubilant, but he couldn't quite get there. Something was nagging at him. It got worse with each passing night, requiring him to drink and dance more and more in hopes of silencing the doubt and worry that plagued his waking hours.

Tonight, he was in a cavernous club in a seedy part of downtown. The room was in the basement of an old brick office building, and the low ceiling was so arrayed with colored lights that it created the sensation of dancing within a kaleidoscope of heavenly bodies. Dio had been dancing for what seemed like hours, yet he did not feel weary, only unsatisfied. He retreated to an area cordoned off with velvet ropes, a space that only he was allowed to occupy—he and whomever he invited into his personal lounge.

Now, he sat alone, damp with sweat, absently holding a glass of red wine with the fingertips of both hands, gazing out over the rhythmically bobbing and gyrating bodies on the packed dance floor. An aerial view would have revealed that the floor was not even near capacity. Yet, from the VIP section where Dio sat, it looked like a full house, because all of the dancers inadvertently gravitated toward him, pressing as close to the velvet ropes as they could. If he rose and went to the unisex bathroom, the mass of partiers would gravitate in that direction, and he would emerge from the facilities to find his way all but blocked. Yet, his way was never truly obscured. The throng of bodies would part for him like the Red Sea for Moses, and he never had to break stride as he moved through the mass of his adoring revellers.

It should have been fun, but Dio was weary of it.

He raised one hand above his head and snapped his fingers. In seconds, a beautiful young woman in a tight miniskirt appeared at his side with an electronic pad on which he scribbled illegibly with his finger. His tab paid, Dio retrieved his leather jacket from where he had tossed it over a leopard skin settee and flung it over his shoulder.

As he walked through the parting cloud, the music faded out as the DJ moved into his next sequence. In the momentary lull, Dio could hear the voices of the clubbers that saw him leaving and reached out to him.

"Don't go," they pleaded. "The night is young and so are we."

They held their arms outstretched and drew their fingers along the silk of his open shirt, along his bare arms, as though they could absorb his power and his beauty through their touch. And perhaps, they could. Those who made contact with him seemed to swoon, their eyes glazing and their lips opening slightly in what amounted to a soundless hymn of praise. Praise to the god of wine, to the high deity of nightlife, to the ecstasy of his rule. Here was his castle and kingdom, here were his subjects, serfs, and ladies in waiting.

As Dio slipped out through the front door and past the bouncers in their dark suits and darker sunglasses, he spoke softly to himself.

"Be young tonight, if you must. For tomorrow and tomorrow and tomorrow you will grow old, and the night will no longer be your lover."

His motorcycle was parked across the street, a BMW S1000 that he'd had built up and customized to the point where it was almost too fast to ride. As he approached his bike, a handful of sequined and bedazzled young women staggered down the sidewalk, coming toward him.

"Hey baby," one called out, teetering dangerously on four-inch heels. "You aren't bailing already, are you? I think you promised me a dance and a shot."

Dio ignored the calls and the whistles, the indecent proposals and pleas. His bike gleamed red in the city lights, and he pulled on his jacket and threw a leg over. The engine screamed to life, and he sat with the clutch held in, twisting the throttle and drowning out the night, the babbling sidewalk drunks, even the thunderous music from inside the club.

In the teardrop-shaped rear-view mirror, he could see the party girls drawing near, stumbling, lurching, reaching for him with red-tipped fingers. It reminded him of a scene from a zombie movie—any zombie movie, really.

Well, he would not be caught tonight. His flesh would feed no ravenous horde.

Dio popped the clutch and twisted the throttle. The front wheel of the bike rose as he accelerated away from the curve, riding a wheelie the length of the block, his open jacket and shirt flapping in the wind, his hair wild and his eyes narrowed.

Behind him, the girls stood blinking, arms limp at their sides, feeling suddenly alone and very sober in the chill of the night.

APOLLO SAT IN THE EXPANSIVE LIVING ROOM AT 12 Mountain View, a bottle of IPA growing warm on the coffee table in front of him, Ebony resting on his knee. He gently plucked at the steel strings with his godly fingertips. He never used a pick. There came from the guitar a succession of mournful and wavering notes, something in the mood of Nirvana, but with more angst and self-loathing than Kurt Cobain could have mustered even at his lowest moments.

Apollo sang softly, but he did not form words. Rather, he hummed and moaned in harmony with his gentle fretwork. The tones of his voice were loaded with mysterious meaning; the effect was something like melodious weeping. As his song went on, he began to handle the strings more roughly, with more urgency, his voice raising with the tempo until he was strumming furiously in a discordant and agonized frenzy, wailing and snarling over the sound of the guitar.

In an instant, he went silent, as though someone had pulled the plug on his mournful and beautiful performance. There were no lights on in the house. Apollo picked up his bottle of beer in darkness and silence.

"Well, that was simply lovely," came a voice from a shadowed corner of the room.

The dark separated itself from the darkness and the human form of Hades took shape. He was merely shadow upon shadow until he struck a match. His face was momentarily ablaze in orange light while he lit a thin black cigar.

"Even the most aggrieved symphonies in the Underworld could not compose a song so wonderfully...bleak," Hades said. "You should come down and give us a performance sometime."

"I decline," Apollo said, his voiced edged with distaste. "I should never play for anyone again, for all eternity."

"Oh, but why?" Hades asked. "You have such power

in your music...power enough even to imprison the King of the Gods himself."

With a sudden motion, Apollo threw the bottle against a wall, where it shattered in an explosion of foam and glass. Hades was laughing before the bottle even reached the wall.

"I cannot believe myself," Apollo moaned. "How many thousands of years will it take for me to no longer be such a fool?"

He leaned forward and held his head in hands, the black Stratocaster sliding to the floor with a metallic thrum. Hades approached, no longer laughing, and sat on the coffee table before his nephew. He lifted Apollo's pack of smokes and shook one loose. Ever so gently, he reached out and placed the cigarette delicately between Apollo's trembling lips. Apollo raised his eyes to look at his uncle, who struck a match with the nail of his thumb and lit the smoke.

"Do not forget, dear nephew, that we had a deal," Hades hissed softly. "You will be paid in full, once the transition is complete. She will be very pleased with you, I can assure you of that."

Dio sped recklessly through the city streets. It was late and traffic was light, but he still had to swerve and dodge around slower moving vehicles, occasionally gunning the bike to get through a light that was somewhere between yellow and red.

He had had a lot to drink, as always. Alcohol did nothing to slow Dio's cognitive processes, it only increased his euphoria momentarily. Most of the pleasure of partying was derived from the way others around him felt and behaved. He would be staggering from the pleasure of watching a rave reach full tilt before he would stumble from drinking a pitcher of wine. He was not a drunk: he was the drunkenness.

Booze did, however, affect his reflexes and reaction time, and he knew that he was putting himself in danger by riding so fast in his condition.

The lights of the city flashed by in a blaze of colors as he whizzed past pawn shops and liquor stores, strip clubs and diners; all the colors of the late-night city scene. The mosaic of light reminded him of the club he had just left, and then he felt as though he was still there, unable to escape the tedium and the crush of the sweating, breathing, expectant throngs.

He twisted the throttle harder.

Finally, he left the neon and halogen of the city behind and steered the bike out into the industrial limits of Toronto, neighborhoods dominated by dark factories and burned-out warehouses. His headlight was the only source of illumination on the inky four-lane blacktop; he felt as though he were able to think about nothing beyond that small and swiftly moving oval of light before him.

He crossed the Don River, black and snake-like beneath the viaduct, the dim lights of a single barge below him, the rumbling of its engines joining his own like a voice from the Underworld.

Dio leaned into sharp curves, his knee nearly grazing the asphalt. He sped along long corridors of chain-link fence that separated massive parking lots from the street, expanses of hard ground for acres around; empty, dark, and quiet.

He drove beneath an overpass that appeared out of the darkness like an apparition and disappeared behind him, the momentary change in the echoes of his bike the only sign that it had even been there.

Dio frowned. He had seen something under the bridge, something pale and pitiful and impossible. Something that was not there, he was almost sure of it, but he throttled down and pulled a U-turn anyway. He had nowhere to be, at any rate.

He approached the overpass more slowly from the other side, squinting into the darkness above to see if there was, in fact, anything up there. In the dark and mist of that small hour, he saw a figure, bound in ropes beneath the cement pillars of the bridge. It was motionless, but undeniably human.

Dio pulled up close to the concrete embankment and killed the motor, glancing in all directions to see if anyone else was around. There was no sign of anyone; no parked cars or lurking shadows, no suggestion of headlights anywhere down the road.

He climbed the slope to the top of the overpass and carefully made his way along the rail. Using the light from his phone, he shined a beam down to see blond hair hanging lank over a young woman's face. She was tied about the shoulders and thighs, hanging upright in such a way that she would be facing eastbound traffic, if there were any. She seemed to be posed in the manner of some ancient sacrifice, like a virgin on the prow of some great ship, commissioned to the gods and bound for the sea. Her eyes were closed and she remained still, but Dio could see that she was breathing.

Dio pulled his knife from his boot. He pressed a button and the blade snapped out of the handle with a click. Reaching down, he cut the ropes that bound the woman's thighs and watched the ropes fall soundlessly to the street below. Then, he reached through the guardrail with his free arm and wrapped it tightly around her waist before sawing through the ropes around her shoulders.

Just as he freed her from the bindings and began to carefully pull her back over the guardrail to safety, the woman moaned and then gasped.

"Easy, easy," he said as she began to flail against him. "I've got you, you're safe now."

The young woman continued to shriek and protest, and Dio was forced to pull her roughly onto the asphalt on his side of the rail. She hit the ground with a grunt and came up fighting.

"No!" she shouted, pounding him on the chest with a closed fist. "No! No!"

Dio backed away, raising his hands in submission before he realized that he still held the switchblade. He immediately folded in the blade and slipped the knife into his jacket pocket.

"I'm not going to hurt you," he said, trying to keep his voice calm. "I found you here and I freed you. So... you're welcome."

"Leave me alone, you stupid drunk!" she shouted.

"Drunk? I'm not drunk!" Dio replied.

Just as the words left his lips, something struck him hard from behind. His world tilted, and the darkness that was all around him, the darkness through which he fled and in which he hid, closed in around his consciousness.

THE CREATURE STOOD BEFORE ZEUS.

It looked almost human. Human, except for the thick blanket of fog that cloaked its body, and the unmoving shadows that concealed its hazy features—an aberration of the light in the form of a human. It had not spoken since Zeus had awakened to find himself shackled and hanging from the side of a cliff. He called out to the creature but received no response.

It simply stood before him, staring.

CHAPTER 3

Dio startled awake, lurching forward and grasping at whatever he could, but he was lost in an endless sea of white. White above, white below, softly luminescent white all around him. The effect was disorienting. He had no idea how long he had been unconscious, and not the slightest clue where he was.

He had sat up too quickly. The hammering blows of pain in his skull reminded him that he had been attacked. Dio lay back with a moan and closed his eyes, his hands stroking his temples. He did not get hangovers, but he imagined that this might be what one felt like. He did not envy his mortal subjects, whom he imagined must often wake in this state after a night of paying him allegiance.

He heard a small sound, a soft shifting of sands or fabrics, and the surface on which he lay yielded slightly to a new weight. He was not alone. He opened his burning eyes and willed his vision to focus. As it did, a face became visible, a woman's head that seemed to float of its own accord.

She had a broad but beautiful face, framed by curls the color of rich earth. As his eyes focused, he saw that her head was not actually floating. She was just dressed in flawless white robes that melded with the white background and gave the impression of her being a... disembodied head (something not completely out of place in the history of the gods). He could see now that he lay in a massive bed, wrapped in white sheets. He could not tell where the soft light was coming from, but the air smelled of the sea.

"Imagine my surprise at finding my prodigal son lying on my front steps this morning," Hera said.

She lifted a bejeweled hand and ran her fingers through Dio's messy hair. He felt a tug as she loosed something dry and crusty from his locks. Blood, he thought.

"You never call your poor, lonely mother, Dionysus. And when I do finally see you, it is because you are drunk and bloodied, passed out in the street like a common *mortal*."

He did not correct her on the use of his ancient name. There was a sense of playful comfort in her voice, and he caught himself leaning affectionately into her touch. He wondered how hard he had been hit.

"I'm sorry," he said, his voice taking a harder edge as

he fought to free himself from his pained and groggy fugue. "I shouldn't have come here."

He rolled away from her and sat up, struggling with the silken sheets that wrapped around his arms and legs, as though they were living entities tasked with keeping him in the bed. Finally, he extracted himself from the bedding and stood in a room of white walls and fluted pillars. A large picture window looked out over an expanse of azure water that he knew was not Lake Ontario, but more likely an apparition, a flawless facsimile of the Aegean Sea. Hera was hopelessly and notoriously homesick. She had been for centuries.

"You're not my mother," he said.

She rose and walked toward the broad window, still watching Dio with a look of both love and guile.

"Fine. Stepmother, then," Hera said. "Yet, here you are, in my home, battered and broken. I have cared for you as a mother would—as a mother *should*. I have not turned you out into the cold, nor have I admonished your foolish ways. Do you not, given these circumstances, think that I might deserve to be called your mother?"

She smiled. Kingdoms had risen and kingdoms had fallen, but Hera's smile had not aged. It still contained all the energy and radiance that one would expect from a goddess.

But Dio was unmoved. He harbored memories of his stepmother that made no sense to him, but were far too powerful, far too painful to be ignored. A shroud protected his mind from what truly happened, of that much he could be certain, but he knew he was young—young even in the mortal sense—and that she had caused him great and grievous pain.

He had vague recollections of her rage, her jealousy. Sometimes he had dreams in which he could see her eyes, filled not with kindness but with hatred; he could see her slender and lovely hands, slick with blood that he knew to be his own. This was all he remembered, but it was enough to keep him from her doorstep. Until now, apparently.

"How did I get here, anyway?" he asked. "The last thing I remember I was on a bridge. There was a girl, and she was in...trouble."

Hera gave a short, scornful laugh. "Trouble," she said, "is exactly what we have now. Thanks to you."

Dio scowled. Hera had turned to gaze out upon the false vista and bask in the impossible Grecian breeze. A peacock strutted into the room, its bold colors even more dazzling in contrast to the stark white of the walls and furnishings. Dio realized he was barefoot and shirtless and began to look around for his things. The headache was already beginning to subside. It was good to be a deity.

"What kind of trouble could I possibly be responsible for?" Dio asked. "I mind my own business. All I did was help a girl that had been tied up and abandoned. Shouldn't I be praised for that? What's more: who hit me? One of *your* henchmen?"

Hera turned from the window and gazed directly at him as he searched about the room. The peacock kept getting in his way; when he tried to shoo it away with his foot, it cried loudly and displayed its wondrous tail, obscuring half the room in a marvelous arc of purple and teal.

Dio looked up to see that Hera's face was now drawn and weary, almost fearful. Something was certainly troubling her, something serious enough to upset the Queen of the Gods.

"The bump on your head is no fault of ours," she said. "Your obnoxious motorbike attracted vagrants and you were mugged. You will find that your wallet is missing. And that girl on the bridge, the one who rescued *you*," she said, her voice taut as a wire, "was not meant to be disturbed."

"Not meant to be *disturbed?*" Dio asked, incredulous. "What are you talking about? What is going on here?"

"You did not recognize her. You wouldn't—you are your father's son, after all. That girl's name is Ari, and she was meant to be on that bridge in the last moments before first light. She would have been there, as promised, if you had not...*rescued* her." Hera's finger pointed to a small door in the corner of the room.

Dio opened it to find that it was a small closet. His shirt had been cleaned and pressed, and his boots were polished.

"Ari?" he asked. "Ari..." The name rang a bell, but he could not quite place it. He had only seen her in the darkness of the previous night, so he could not be sure if he recognized her. "And you say she was *supposed* to be there? Tied up like that? What in the Underworld is going on, Hera?"

Hera winced at the sound of her name from Dio's lips. They had a complicated past, to be sure, but she had long desired that he think of her as his mother, and he had long declined.

"She was a willing sacrifice," Hera said, her voice trembling uncharacteristically. "She was promised to The Darkness, as a means of achieving peace and safety for another season. We are merely trying to protect the mortals."

She walked to a white chair in the corner of the room and collapsed into it, seeming suddenly very tired. Dio had pulled on his shirt and now sat on the foot of the white bed to lace his boots.

"Are you into this 'Darkness' stuff like my father was?" he asked, irritated at how pained and bratty his voice sounded in that moment.

"What do you mean, 'was'?" Hera asked, leaning forward in the chair.

"Zeus has been MIA for, like, months. You didn't know?"

Hera let out a long breath and fell back in the chair once again. She brought her jewel-covered hands to her face and rubbed her eyes, then spoke through a web of fingers.

"We haven't exactly kept in touch in recent years,

ever since I decided to move out of the house on Mountain View."

Hera had taken up other residence once she finally grew tired of Zeus' constant hero fantasies. She had said, in one particular moment of exasperation, that it was like living with a schizophrenic who thought that every day was Halloween. And though Zeus' power to truly command the gods had disappeared, Hera had chosen to remain in Toronto: *Olympians should stick together. We are a big Greek family, after all.*

"But," she went on, "I did not know that he was missing."

She dropped her hands in her lap and stared hard at Dio.

"You say that he had spoken of a darkness as well? He was aware?"

Dio shrugged, feeling more and more uncomfortable with the situation.

"He was aware of something, I guess. He was always going on about The Darkness closing in or getting closer or whatever. He would ramble about some unspeakable evil from ancient myths."

"Not from myth," Hera said. "But from memory. You must remember, Dio, that 'myth' is just a word that mortals use to describe history that their feeble minds cannot comprehend."

He had heard something to that effect before, from his father.

"Zeus' disappearance is very bad news, very bad

indeed," Hera said. "For if he was right, and if *I* am right, then we will be in need of his power."

Dio was casually trying to make his way to the door, hoping that he would be able to navigate his own way out of Hera's massive home. Then he stopped and turned to fix his stepmother with a curious gaze.

"Are you trying to tell me that all this 'Darkness' shit is legitimate? That Zeus hasn't completely lost his mind?"

Hera rose and glided across the room on silent feet, having regained some of her usual grace and composure.

"Son, the enemy that we now face is as real as you or me, and considerably older," she said. "If your father has gone missing, it is most certainly related to what is going on. It is imperative that you find him and discover how to stop The Darkness."

Dio raised his hands, palms forward toward his stepmother.

"Whoa, whoa, whoa. Me?" he protested. "I didn't ask to be a part of this. This seems like something that you old timers are more qualified for. This in none of my business."

"On the contrary!" Hera exclaimed, her voice now loud and stern. She pointed a slender finger directly at Dio's face. "It was *you* who removed our sacrifice from the bridge. *You* who brought riffraff trailing you onto the sacred grounds. *You* who allowed your father to be taken away from us, without a thought! So, it is *your* responsibility to see that this gets sorted out, or we do not know what will become of the mortals." Hera took a breath and collected herself, shrinking back down to size from the stature that her anger had bequeathed her.

"And, as you probably know," she added, her voice now somber, "if the mortals are in danger, so too are we."

Dio had heard the rumors all his life, that the existence of the pantheon was dependent upon the memory of the people. He had once thought that connection to be metaphorical, but now, looking into the forlorn eyes of the Queen of the Gods, he wondered if it might be more literal than he ever would have dared to imagine.

When he spoke again, he did so with a humility he had not known in many years.

"What...what is expected of me?"

Hera almost smiled, though Dio thought she looked too sad and weary to manage it.

"Find your father," she said. "Discover from him the nature of The Darkness and help him to defeat it."

Dio looked to the floor. In contrast with the pure white of the carpeting, his boots looked like twin pools of spilled oil.

"I am not a hero, like my father," he said. "I'm just a god of wine and good times. The sun does not rise for me, nor would lightning ever heed my command. I fear I am not up to such a task."

Hera reached out, and with the gentlest of touches, raised his chin until his eyes met hers.

"You will have help," she told him. "Just follow the twine."

She turned and walked back to the window that looked out over a sea that was thousands of miles away. Dio opened his mouth to ask her what she meant, but by the way that she stood and the look in her eyes, he could tell that she would say nothing more to him. He turned and silently left the room.

In the corridor, he found that the end of a length of twine had been tied to the doorknob. It trailed for a great distance through the house and then angled to the right and disappeared. Perplexed, Dio followed it.

The twine stretched and bent and weaved through the mansion, at times wrapped around banisters or ancient pieces of gleaming armor, leading down a spiral staircase and finally through a library and into a courtyard in the rear of the estate. The twine dropped across the sun-drenched lawn and disappeared into a structure, built mostly of glass, that reminded Dio very much of his greenhouse at home, except that this space was entirely void of flora.

He carefully opened the door and stuck his head inside. In the center of the room, a young woman lay sprawled on a chaise lawn chair. Her hair was a strawberry blond, very long and frizzy, and she was draped in a flowing lavender robe. The sun shone through the glass roof of the building, and she luxuriated in its rays, though her skin was white as porcelain and one might think she would burn very easily.

"Oh? You're awake..." She spoke without turning her head toward Dio. "You went down pretty easy for a god." Her eyes and half of her face were hidden behind an oversized pair of sunglasses, but Dio recognized the voice immediately as the girl from the bridge...the sacrifice.

"You must be Ari," he said, feeling awkward.

She turned her head slightly in his direction and lowered her shades, showing brilliant green eyes, bright and bemused.

"You wouldn't remember me, would you?" she said. He sensed that it was not a question she intended him to answer. "I suppose that may be for the better. So, I am told that I'm supposed to help you."

"I guess so," he said weakly. Dio wished that there were flowers in this hothouse. He always felt more comfortable around flowers.

"Well, pretty boy," Ari said, "let's get something straight: I am not a face. Do you know what that means?"

He shook his head.

"It means that I help from the periphery. I don't get my hands dirty. You let me know what you need, keep me in the loop, and I use my connections to see things through, but don't be expecting me to go charging into battle with you."

"Battle?" Dio asked, feeling suddenly very small.

Ari made a vague gesture. "Metaphorically. Probably. Don't worry, god of grapes. It'll be fine." A quick motion of her hand shushed Dio before he could correct her.

With her other hand, she punched a series of commands into a phone that he had not noticed until now. Dio's phone suddenly vibrated in his pocket. He jumped. The muggers must not have realized he was carrying it.

"Now you have my digits," Ari said. "Hit me up when you figure out what you're doing."

She slid her sunglasses back into place and lay back again, apparently done with the conversation. Dio turned to the door and began to leave, had a thought, and turned back to the girl.

"Can I ask you a question?"

"Shoot."

"Hera said you were a willing sacrifice to The Darkness. Is that true?"

Ari was motionless besides a drumming of her fingers on the arms of the chair. A movement that belied impatience with this questioning.

"If the boss lady said it, then it's true."

Dio ran his fingers through his hair and squinted in the bright sun.

"If you were a willing sacrifice, then why did you have to be tied up?" he asked.

Ari turned her head once again toward Dio and lowered her sunglasses, fixing him with a gaze that could have been curious, but he felt was more likely incredulous.

"You ever been a living sacrifice before, party boy?" she asked.

He shook his head, though he knew the real answer was more complicated.

"Well, let me tell you," Ari said. "It involves a lot of second thoughts."

CHAPTER 4

Dio left the manor to find the morning surprisingly warm. It was the kind of still, humid dawn that foretold a sweltering day; he unbuttoned his shirt halfway down his chest before slipping on his dark sunglasses.

A manservant at the front door of Hera's house had told him where to find his motorcycle, explaining cryptically that they did not want it parked in front of the estate, attracting "unwanted attention." Dio was unclear about what this meant, but his head was already too filled with mysteries and puzzles, so he refrained from inquiring and walked toward downtown, where his bike was to be parked in front of the Fairmont Royal York hotel, a venue that had the sort of old-world charm that ageless beings might feel at home in.

Morning was typically not his time, but for once,

Dio was glad for the hour and the excuse to walk. He had been ignoring the conditions of his life for some time now, refusing to worry about Zeus' disappearance or the increasing murmurs about The Darkness. It seemed now that his fate was catching up to him. He had to do more than drink and dance and sleep and brood. He had to be a god again.

The sky was bright and pale yellow through a high skein of clouds, the color almost white and somehow foreboding. As Dio descended from the heights of the lavish neighborhood where Hera had made her home into the brick and mirror corridors of downtown Toronto, he sensed a presence moving with him, something remote but attentive. Several times he looked back, turning quickly to catch any would-be stalker off guard, but the street behind him was empty of threats. Besides the usual traffic of commuters, the only things that seemed to be moving on this hot and silent morning were three vultures that circled high above and behind Dio, their large wingspans silhouetted black against the pale sky.

Dio considered it fortunate that Hera's people had chosen to leave his bike in front of a hotel, because he was hungry and still a bit groggy. He desired coffee and a pastry from a stellar cafe. He wondered idly if Hera had anticipated this, if it was her odd way of looking after him. He was disappointed, however, upon arriving at the hotel and finding the cafe closed. A small sign announced this fact without offering a reason, and Dio's eyes lingered for a long moment on the length of twine that had been used to bind together the brass door handles at the entrance.

As he turned to walk back into the street, where his motorcycle waited, a woman's voice echoed across the open courtyard that claimed the space between the cafe and the lobby.

"Sir! Sir!" she called. "The cafe is closed today, but there are coffee and pastries in the lobby!"

What luck, Dio thought. *Perhaps today won't be such a rough one after all.*

The lobby had incredibly high ceilings and ornate chandeliers. There were clusters of armchairs and elegant sofas here and there, arranged around gleaming coffee tables on oriental rugs. As Dio stirred cream and sugar into his coffee and selected a pastry from a silver platter, he heard what sounded like a pig snorting.

The sound was so out of place in that rich setting that he could not help but investigate. Shortly, he found the source of the muffled snorting. A very old, very short man was nestled deeply into an enormous wing-back chair. His head was tilted to one side and his mouth hung open. Every few seconds his chest would heave slightly as his mouth emitted a shuddering snore.

Something about the man gave Dio a strange sense of pause. He found that he could not simply walk away and leave the old man to his nap, so he sat down in the chair across from him to attend to his breakfast and see what might happen.

The old man wore a well-tailored suit of the deepest blue, with a matching tie and a powder blue shirt. There was a red poppy pinned to his lapel, and his shoes were of perfectly polished brown leather. Even in his slumbering state, everything about him spoke of fastidiousness. Every hair was in place. He was freshly shaven, and he emitted a faint odor of lavender and vanilla.

The wide double doors leading out onto the street swung open, and a prim-looking woman hurried into the lobby, dragging behind her a screaming boy of about seven. As the mother and son made their way to the elevators on the other end of the cavernous room, the racket roused the old man somewhat. His head jerked from one side to the other and his regular breathing was interrupted. He sniffed, then his eyes fluttered for a moment, regarding Dio with a sleepy stare. With a yawn, the man lifted a hand to his mouth, and Dio noticed the letters "HYPN" tattooed across the knuckles. The tattoos were skillfully done, the letters almost dainty, but the effect of the markings on this refined old man was still striking. Immediately, Dio understood who…what…was before him.

"Curses," the man muttered, his voice thick with sleep. "I can hardly wait for the endless night."

This was Hypnos, the primordial deity of sleep. Primordial deities—beings older than the Olympians—were not just gods. They were elements, ideas, and places unto themselves. Similarly, Hypnos was more than just a god of sleep; he was sleep incarnate.

His eyes closed again, and his head bobbed forward. Dio, hearing these words, sat forward and put his coffee cup down on the table.

"Endless night?" he said, trying to speak quietly enough to not attract the attention of the hotel clerks and bellhops scattered around the lobby, but loudly enough to coax the old man back to wakefulness, if that was possible.

"Hey, old fella, what did you say about endless night?" he tried again.

Hypnos grunted, his old mouth curling into a wry smile, though his eyes remained closed.

"Yes...the never-ending night...so I can sleep eternally, without being bothered by these mortals and their trifling problems..." He trailed off and began to snore softly.

Dio got up and moved close to the side of the chair where Hypnos slumbered.

"The Darkness," he whispered into his ear. "What is it?"

Hypnos' reply could have been some fragment of a dream he was experiencing, or a whisper of a memory, he said it so faintly, as though the word was nothing more than the breath of sleep.

"*Mother.*"

"Don't do anything stupid" said Hades, his eyes glowing white, fuelled by the power of the Underworld.

Apollo stood before him in a cold sweat. He could see the silhouette of his father in the distant darkness, a grey figure surrounded by small flecks of light.

"Let me at least speak to him."

"No."

"Uncle, please." Apollo pleaded. "He's my father."

"And what's that got to do with anything?" Hades' voice was severe. "Remember why you're here, boy."

The Underworld was a strange place—not a place of fire and brimstone, but a bastion of despair, and helplessness, and memory. A voice called out repeatedly to Apollo. Someone from the past, a love never forgotten...a crime never forgiven.

You did this to me, God of the Sun.

Apollo stepped forward. He could feel Zeus' pain. But could Zeus feel his? The gods had lived thousands of years, and in a thousand years lived loss and regret. He had hoped he could right a wrong; at that moment, he began to understand that retribution was not one action. It was more than undoing a wrong. It was repairing a wrong.

This act had repaired nothing.

"Uncle," Apollo said. "This is wrong. I made a mistake. *We've* made a mistake. We have to let my father go. What would you do if it were your son, Zagreus?"

"And what of your sweet Daphne? Would you have her continue to rot for your mistakes?" His white eyes seemed to burn brighter as he smiled. "I can assure you, her time here has not been pleasant." He raised his palm, a sickly green sphere formed, and Apollo felt a cold wind blow dust and fragments of rock and bone toward him; he raised his arm to shield his eyes, and he remembered Daphne's face—her radiant smile. The smile that had once turned to screams as Apollo—enchanted and fuelled by lust—chased her relentlessly through forests surrounding her home. Ultimately, the nymph had only one escape.

When he lowered his arm, the dust had settled to reveal an ancient tree, one Apollo knew all too well. A laurel tree. As he looked harder, he saw Daphne, chained to it, as she had been for millennia. A spiteful voice spoke to Apollo from her dead, soundless, lips.

Look at me. Look at me. One thousand years I have withered. Know that one thousand more I would wither if it meant never having to see you again. Why won't you die, Apollo?

"Daphne..."

Even the sound of my name from you hurts me. Get away from me!

"Please listen to me! I didn't know...I love you—"

The voice shrieked, and somewhere in the background Apollo heard a chorus of laughter—Hades, and another. But before he was able to turn, his vision left him. Sound left him. His strength left him. Even his golden voice left him. Deaf, dumb, and blind, Apollo fell to his knees, struggling to breathe. Something was different. This was not blindness—this was the absence of light, or sound, or air. A blackness, thick and tangible, took from him his senses.

The bottom of a shoe pressed against the side of his head, and he collapsed to the grey floor.

"Zagreus"—a voice said—"was an impertinent little shit."

DIO X ARI I

DIO: Hi. You'll never guess who I ran into today.

ARI: Who is this?

DIO: Umm, it's Dio. You gave me your number.

...

DIO: Earlier at Hera's place.

ARI: Oh, of course. How's it going, your holy grapeliness?

DIO: You do know that I'm more than just a god of wine, right?

ARI: Sure, sure, you do that gardening thing nobody cares about.

DIO: I'm pretty sure the farmers care.

ARI: Not since they figured out pesticide and fertilizer, honey.

...

DIO: Right. So. I was saying I met someone today. Someone peculiar.

ARI: Did he look like the little old man from *Up*?

DIO: ...So you knew.

ARI: Of course I knew. Why do you think we left your bike there?

DIO: Do you know anything else then? Anything about The Darkness?

...

DIO: You still there?

ARI: I know that whatever it is, it's hungry.

DIO: I think I know where to find someone who might have some answers.

ARI: That's great. Who?

DIO: Probably better we don't say his name. He has a way of showing up places.

ARI: Might I make a suggestion, oh lord of the grapevine?

DIO: *sighs* Yes.

ARI: Leave the bike at home. Drunk driving is a real turn off. Even when it's you. Besides, it's a nice night to take a walk along the river. Don't you think?

DIO: I guess it is. Perhaps...you'd care to join me?

...

DIO: Hello?

CHAPTER 5

That evening, Dio left the house at 12 Mountain View just as dusk was beginning to descend over Toronto. Uncharacteristically, he had asked Apollo to join him. But Apollo—drunk and lost in alcohol and cigarette smoke—told Dio to disappear. "That's all you're ever good for," he had said. And Dio had thought it best to oblige.

The day had finally gone from pale yellow to a burning pink, heat still shimmering on the streets, creating a thick haze over the waters.

Dio was responding to an invitation, which was not something he normally did. True, he received dozens of invitations every weekend via various social media outlets. Mortals who were familiar with his reputation invited him to all manner of parties and soirees, ranging from the benign to the macabre. Anyone who had ever partied with him before wanted him to attend their gatherings, their tiny bacchanals. The invitations amounted to whatever was left of the cult of Dionysus, the strange and ragged ends of his former glory. That is why he ignored them: the invitations and the sad affairs to which they were attached only reminded him of how far he had fallen.

This night, however, he broke with custom and was heading across town to a rave. His purpose in going had less to do with dancing and partying and more to do with the guest list. Dio had it on good authority that someone would be in attendance with whom he wished to speak, and this might be the only time to catch the elusive man of the night.

As he approached the water of the Don River, Dio saw that the three vultures still circled him, black shapes in the gathering night. A ferry boat was moored on the lapping banks of the river, and Dio boarded and paid his fare. The ferryman wore a name tag that read "Charlie," and Dio recognized him, not by his face, but by the way he plied the waters with a solemn and grave sense of duty.

Dio was the only passenger on the ferry. Before he disembarked on the far bank, he spoke to Charlie, glancing around at the darkening shadows as he did.

"What do you make of all this, Charon?" he asked. "Have you heard the rumors? Or are you able to sense it yourself, the coming Darkness?"

Charon leaned against the door to the wheelhouse and gazed out over the obsidian waters of the Don. The city lights reflected and distorted upon the rippling surface, creating an alternate world that was distinctly different, yet utterly the same.

"You know how much my work means to me, don't you, Dionysus?" he said.

Dio bristled at the use of his full name, the name so inextricably tied to his former greatness, but he did not protest Charon's use of it. No one protested much of anything that Charon did. The boatman of the Styx was untouchable—older perhaps than the gods themselves, and indifferent to their needs.

"Yes, everyone knows that you take your duties very seriously," Dio replied. "And might I add that you are doing a great job here. You run a tight ship, as they say." He smiled coyly. "How'd you even get this job? Like, did you sit around an office and tell some primordial administrative assistant that you're looking for an offshore position?"

Charon turned to look Dio full in the face for the first time.

"Do not mock me, you sniveling wino," he spat. "You know nothing of creation; nothing of erasure. Pathetic gods, yearning for glory, living weakly on what remnants of worship you find in the memories of mortals. I am the boatman. Whether your kind light the fires of life or be extinguished, I will still be the boatman."

Dio held his hands up, palms out.

"Take it easy, Charlie...I didn't mean anything by it.

You know how I am. Drunken revelry, life of the party, and all that. But what are you talking about? Dude, what do you mean by 'extinguished'?"

Charon only stood before him, silent. After a long moment, the boatman gestured slightly toward a grassy patch of shore. Dio nodded, stepped off the ferry, and walked along into the night without looking back.

DIO X ARI II

DIO: So I saw Charon. He was his "charming" self.

ARI: I think he's just peachy.

DIO: And not very helpful.

ARI: A girl could get lost thinking about tall primordial creatures that spend all their time on the water...*swoon*

DIO: Hah. Right. So. I've been meaning to ask you something...

ARI: Anything, handsome. For you, I'm an open book.

DIO: Do I know you from somewhere?

ARI: I don't know. Do you?

DIO: I'm being serious. Have we met before?

ARI: I think you'd remember having met me.

DIO: Something about you just feels so...familiar.

ARI: Are you calling me forgettable?

DIO: No, of course not. Sorry. It's been a long day.

ARI: Sure it has. Well, if there's nothing else, I have things to do.

DIO: What exactly is it that you do?

ARI: Oh, you know. Maiden stuff...walk alone, cry on beaches, wait to be rescued by handsome deities. That sort of thing.

DIO: I get the feeling that I've upset you somehow...

ARI: No, Dio. Not at all.

DIO: Are you sure?

...

DIO: Hello?

CHAPTER 6

Dio felt the rave before he heard it. The pavement beneath his boots began to quake with a rhythmic intensity. He surveyed his surroundings in the partying heart of the city, and noticed several passages leading underground. There was a subway entrance, a couple of steaming manholes, and a flight of stairs that led to an establishment below street level.

The party wouldn't be in the subway. Too many cops. The manholes were unlikely, though not impossible; he had once been to a rager in a derelict section of the Parisian sewer system. He decided to check out the stairs first and was confronted at the landing by a hulking bouncer.

"You on the list?" the man asked. He was dressed all in black, wore sunglasses even in the murky stairwell, and outweighed Dio by at least one hundred and fifty pounds.

"I'm on every list, my friend. I'm the damn letterhead."

The bouncer looked down at the clipboard in his hand and then back at Dio. A certain type of unsteady wrath lurked behind the shades.

"It's a rave, Goliath," Dio said. "Every poor sap you turn away is one less body in there rolling and making money for your boss, which is...I'm gonna guess, Giuseppe? Or is this a House of Lee production? Either way, you leave me out on the street, they're going to hear about it, and you're going to be looking for a job blocking some other door in a crappier part of town. I was invited. Get out of my way."

The giant hesitated only a second before reaching over and shoving the door open for Dio. Sure, Dio could have given him his name, or even just leaned in and sent the guy into some ecstatic frenzy that he would never understand as more than a headache and a broken heart in the morning, but what was the sport in that? Dio wanted to stand up for the little guy by playing the part of the little guy.

Inside, the bass line threatened the pulse of everyone packed into the sprawling basement space. Concussive electric percussion elevated heart rates, burst eardrums, and guided bodies to twist and step.

Streaks of blue and green light slashed through the darkness as black-clad, jaded ravers slashed the air with glow sticks, wielding their luminescent accessories like weapons. Grown men gnawed on pacifiers while they convulsed to the music. Women sweated and writhed, grinding their sneakers and boots on the gritty cement floor as the pulsating lights made their pale skin glow in the way of fallen angels.

Dio scanned the crowd, not looking at faces, but rather looking for aberrations in the crush of humanity that filled the basement. Those with divine connections tended to disrupt the patterns of normal, mortal interaction. For example, right now, Dio was attracting ravers like a porch light attracts night insects. The dancers didn't consciously move closer to Dio; their seemingly random and enraptured steps pulled them into his proximity. From the moment Dio had entered, he was constantly on the move lest he become trapped in a tangled mass of bodies, a cage of inebriated adoration.

But the aberration that Dio looked for was different, almost the antithesis of his legendary allure.

And before long, he found it.

In the middle of the expansive dance floor was a chasm of open space, as though the earth itself had opened and swallowed all those who had danced there moments before, pushing the others to its outer limits, oblivious and bobbing as though in a deep trance. The only thing that made it clear that there was a space capable of being danced upon was the shape of a lean and limber man, his long, blond hair glowing in the blacklight.

This god inhabited the body of a young man, only about the age that Dio had taken on, and he danced in a way that would have set him apart from the crowd even if they had not been avoiding him. He would lean back to face to the ceiling, then drop forward with such grace and certainty that he looked like a professional diver, throwing his body toward the floor. His knees would buckle, and his heels would slide apart. He was swan diving into the cement floor, barely keeping his feet, but doing so with such dark beauty that it rivaled any professional interpretive dancer on any stage in the world.

The dancer was tall, angular, shirtless, with sweat-soaked, dripping long hair, the blond darkened with moisture and falling over his bony shoulders to frame the mosaic of tattoos on his chest. Across his breast were bright whorls of fire, gashes of blue sky punctuated with clouds and overseen by a golden sun. There were luminous figures soaring up one ribcage, and dark, shadowy beings clamoring down the other. But the central image, the one that seemed to be the oldest, was a tall and vicious scythe, the handle of which reached from his navel to his left collarbone, where it met the blade that reached across his chest and came to a vicious point just beneath his left armpit. Beneath his navel, in broad, dark letters above his pants line was tattooed one word: "Thanatos."

For ten meters in every direction, the floor around Thanatos was wide open. Despite his skilled and mesmerizing dance moves, the other ravers avoided the slender dancer as though a foul stench circled him, as though he carried with him a forcefield that repelled every living thing.

Casually, Dio slid into the chasm that separated Thanatos from the rest of the dancers. He moved across the void, swaying easily with the rhythms of the thunderous bass line, affecting the hooded eyes and dismissive gait of the other partiers. He approached Thanatos and ducked in close to Death, moving in tandem with his counterpart. Thanatos opened his eyes and looked at Dio, the smallest trace of a smile playing at one corner of his mouth. He contorted his body backward and forward, looking as though he were in the throes of some incredible possession from which he never wanted to recover. Dio matched his every move in reverse, lunging forward when Thanatos arched back, and bending back when Death bent into him.

After some moments of this gracefully painful dance, Dio addressed his partner.

"I talked to your brother today," Dio said. "He says something...someone...is coming. What can I expect?"

Thanatos continued to dance, sweat running down his lithe and pale body.

"You who have always walked in the light never learned to hold your tongues," Thanatos shouted over the music. "Your questions will only lead you to the depths, and there, Cerberus will tear you into a thousand pieces. So shut up and dance with me."

Dio smirked. He had expected Thanatos' defiance. He knew that all he had to do was walk away, and the specter of death would be left to dance away his night in absolute solitude, impossibly alone in a room full of people.

Instead of leaving, Dio began to dance in his own way, his momentum carrying his body from side to side rather than front to back. He was stone sober, but the action made his head swim subtly with something like intoxication. The new moves were not for Thanatos, but for those mortals who formed the wide ring around the empty center of the dance floor.

Little by little, ravers began to dance into the chasm, unsteady, off center, and seemingly drunk. Thanatos watched the dancers approach, nearly expressionless, the circle shrinking in on him. Once the first dancer reached the space where Dio and Thanatos writhed and gyrated together, the music accelerated in tempo and swelled in volume, and Thanatos at last began to grin.

He had a wide grin, as if he had somehow eaten the crescent moon.

A young man threw himself over Thanatos' shoulder, his chin resting on the tip of the tattooed scythe. A female raver slid into the space in front of him, drawing her thumbs across the tattoo above his belt. Thanatos grinned wickedly at Dio.

"I wish you would come out more often," he said. "For some reason, these wretched mortals won't come near me normally."

Despite all their foolhardy ways, the mortals remain afraid to dance with death, Dio thought. *Perhaps, beneath everything, they still feel they have something to live for.*

Dio continued to dance, even as he slowly and methodically separated himself from the growing throng of dancers in the middle of the floor. Soon, Thanatos was surrounded by a thick and surging ring of humanity; heads bobbing, knees bending, all moving in tandem with his esoteric movements.

"I'm glad you're having fun," Dio shouted over the heads of Thanatos' new supplicants. "Perhaps you could return the favor."

A PALE HAND RAN ALONG ZEUS' CHEST. HIS EYES weary, and his mind muddled, it took him a moment to focus on the woman floating before him. She was laughing, relishing her time with the King of the Gods—the way one would with a loved one on a breezy summer's day. Yet, the land around Zeus was not illuminated by the warm rays of summer, and her hair hung limp in the dead air.

"You," he deigned. He knew her name, it was there —somewhere—in his ancient consciousness, yet his lips could not form the sounds to speak it. "You are The Darkness."

She met his words with a smile. Ran her hand along the side of his face. Her name continued to elude him, yet who she was—*what* she was—was becoming slowly clearer. She was the ancient night, so old that even the Olympians thought her a tale. One of the eldest primordial gods. But what was her name?

"The Darkness?" her voice seethed. Like a brook that somehow trickled over a bed of lava. "It was always only a matter of time before the mortals would forget you. But I am surprised that your kind could forget me."

"You clearly didn't make much of an impression!" Zeus smiled, silently congratulating himself for maintaining his sense of humor. Sure, it had been hundreds of years since he was last strapped to a cliff face, yet he was certain that help was coming. It had been months before he felt it, but someone was looking for him. A god. Just the thought of it made him feel more powerful.

The woman floated closer to Zeus, her breath heavy and warm on the old king's face. As if she could feel the flicker of hope ignited in his being, she spoke. "My daughters flock to your weakest child. Soon they will feast on his miserable carcass."

"Call them off, creature." Zeus struggled and strained at his manacles; he willed lightning to strike, yet neither divine strength nor mystical might came to him.

The floating woman smiled. It was then that Zeus realized that this creature was more than just dark night distilled into a being. It was the dark night distilled into a being he once loved. As he examined her face closer, he found the features of Semele—Dio's mortal mother—twisted and warped. Where Semele's smile was summer air, the floating woman's lips held only pain and despair. Semele's voice had been dipped gently in honey; the floating woman's had been soaked in vinegar. Their eyes were most different of all, for the creature had none—just two endless pits.

Zeus could not imagine a more painful sight, and his body hung weakly once more.

"Was it you, creature? Were you the one that—"

"—That whispered into the ear of your dear, sweet Semele?" The Darkness cackled, and the atmosphere around Zeus crackled to life.

───※───

THANATOS SPRAWLED ACROSS THE RED VELVET cushions of the VIP booth. He was damp with sweat and exhausted, though joy and contentment possessed his features. He spoke to Dio like a man drunk with wine.

"Of course my brother would be napping in a hotel lobby," he said, gesturing grandly with his hands. He had long and slender fingers, adorned with many rings. His wrists were heavy with bracelets of all manner; Dio noticed that amongst the diamonds and precious metals, some were simple scraps of twine, wound and knotted around Thanatos' bony wrists.

"All the money in the world, and that old crank Hypnos doesn't even get himself a room," he went on.

"He seemed comfortable enough to me," Dio remarked.

"Oh, and I am sure he was!" Thanatos cried. The deep thump of the bass was still loud enough in this private corner that they had to raise their voices. "He can catch a wink anywhere, I tell you! He once fell asleep on the subway and missed his stop so many times that security called the police. They thought he was living on the train. Once, back in 1912, he fell asleep on the deck of a cruise ship. The ship sank, and he didn't wake up until he was being pulled from the freezing water by rescuers! It's all true! I was there!"

"Oh? And what were you doing there?"

"Do you really need to ask?" Thanatos tilted his head back and laughed at the ceiling, his thin, tattooed chest heaving with the motion. Dio waited patiently for him to return from his memories. Some of the ravers, drawn by Dio's power, had gravitated closer to the booth, dancing rhythmically and unconsciously in their direction. Thanatos paused to watch them, a wistful look in his eyes.

"You really have it made, Dio," he said. "You always have. God of wine and merriment. Prince of parties. Deity of debauchery. What do I have? I get to represent the ultimate and final end of all that fun. It's no wonder that no one will dance with me; I stand for everything they fear, everything they spend all their time and money trying to escape. I should have been you, Dio. I would have made the world into a party."

"You do realize that I'm more than just a god of wine, right? Farmers worshipped me—"

"No one cares! Why don't you go and be Death for a while? Let me enjoy myself for a change."

Dio knew that Thanatos was speaking hypothetically, drunk and feeling sorry for himself, but it gave him an idea.

"Sure," he said. "I'll let you run the party circuit for a spell. Give me your key to the Underworld, and I'll hold down the fort for you."

Thanatos snickered, then stopped when he saw the expression on Dio's face.

"What? Are you serious?" he asked. "You would give up your powers and go under? Are we even able to do something like that? Swap out powers, I mean."

Dio leaned forward, setting his wine glass on the low table between them. He didn't care for this vintage. Californian wines always tasted too young to his palate. He much preferred old-world reds to these West Coast whites. He missed Greece.

"I have no interest in your abilities, Than, and I'm pretty sure we can't trade off anyway. But I think I could manage to give you some sway, for a little while, if you want to take a break from being a lonely pariah."

Thanatos scowled across the table and seemed about to say something before being interrupted by a beautiful young woman who suddenly appeared behind him. She began running her fingers over his shoulders and down his chest as she rested her face against his neck. Thanatos turned to stone at the first touch before melting into the seat, his eyes closed in the ecstasy of simple human contact. What Thanatos could not see was that the woman's eyes were focused solely on Dio.

"Don't play me for a fool, Dio," Thanatos said, eyes still closed as the woman doted on him with drunken affection. "I know that you're looking for Zeus. I heard you were on the bridge too—poking your nose where it doesn't belong."

"Which is it then?" Dio's voice seemed suddenly gruff. "Am I looking for my father, or am I meddling in affairs that aren't my business? Because the location and condition of my father are facts that most certainly *are* my business, wouldn't you agree?"

Dio was taken aback by his own words and tone. He could not remember the last time that he spoke of his father with anything besides resentment. To make demands now, to speak brusquely to Death, in order to learn the whereabouts of his father—he decided that it had been a very long and strange couple of days.

Thanatos was looking at him closely now, measuring him. The girl was gone as mysteriously as she had appeared. Somewhere in the far reaches of the dark club, the DJ flipped a switch, and the music went suddenly silent. The crowd of ravers roared and whistled, begged for more. In a long, tense moment where nothing filled the air around them but darkness and mortal cries, two ancient ones studied one another.

"You cannot stop what is happening, Dionysus. *We* are nothing like you Olympians. We do not live or wither based on the pathetic remembrance of our names. Mortals pray to me simply by doing what they do best." Thanatos smiled his wicked smile. "Dying."

As he spoke, Thanatos reached into the pocket of his leather pants and withdrew a small object. "They pray to Mother any time their eyes strain to see the dark. And Hypnos? The mortals pray to him most of all...pity he's too sleepy to ever do anything with all that power." His eyes were wide now. "You Olympians, a bunch of so-called gods. You're little more than mortals failing at most basic requisite of mortality. This moment has been approaching for millennia, and you are a powerless god."

"We're not entirely powerless, Thanatos."

"Who amongst your kind truly has power? To transform, to battle, to command the elements. None. Time has favored us. The time of Olympians and mortals has come to an end."

Thanatos leaned forward and set the object in the middle of the table. It was a semicircle of gold, one half of a coin, engraved about the edges in a language from time immemorial.

"But, since your mission is futile, I may as well have a little fun," Thanatos said.

"Where is the other half?" Dio demanded, nodding toward the split coin.

Thanatos, feigning surprise, spread his hands wide.

"What, you didn't think I possessed the entire key, did you?" he laughed. "Of course not. You'll have to get that from Erebus. I think you know where to find him."

Dio pressed his fingertips into his forehead. He felt the beginnings of a headache. Eventually, he reached forward and picked up the coin, then rose to his feet.

"Uh, uh, uh," Thanatos chided, grabbing Dio's wrist. "We had a deal, did we not?"

Dio looked down, hoping that his expression transmitted the disgust and annoyance he felt toward Thanatos at that moment.

"We did indeed."

The music began again as the DJ at last dropped the beat. Out of the darkness came throngs of sweating dancers, male and female, of every race, color, and creed. They pushed through the velvet ropes of the VIP area just as Dio ducked out. The last he heard from Thanatos, before the thunderous music drowned out his voice, was a cruel and rapturous laughter.

※

A FULL, WHITE MOON SHONE DOWN ON TORONTO'S streets as Dio left the underground club. From its angle, almost perfectly situated in the top of the sky, it cast nearly no shadows on the earth. A halo of its own reflected light encompassed the moon; as Dio gazed up, he could see the shapes of three dark creatures, circling within that ring of luminescence. The vultures had not left him since he departed his stepmother's house the previous morning. Perhaps he should have felt worried —vultures after all, were birds of prey—but with his father missing, and some unknown force on the brink of attack, clingy vultures were the least of his problems.

He headed west, walking through pools of light evenly distributed from bowing streetlamps. He had to again cross the Don as he made his way toward the St. James Town neighbourhood. Charlie was no longer there, and neither was his ferry. As Dio crossed the river using a small unkempt footpath, he found himself both curious and relieved. Something about the boatman always made him uncomfortable.

ZEUS JERKED AND THRASHED HIS BODY, WHIPPING HIS head from side to side trying, unsuccessfully, to break free. Below him was a small object of ash and light. He had seen it before, but now it was moving toward him. Very carefully.

It was nearing three in the morning when Dio approached St. James Cemetery. The oxidized, green steeple of the chapel glowed in the moonlight like some alien monolith. The gates were closed but easily climbed, and as Dio swung his leg over the top of the wrought iron fence, cursing himself for not staying in better shape, he thought he heard singing coming from deep within the heart of the graveyard.

It was a small voice, high and mournful, and Dio followed it into the inky depths of the cemetery. Though lanterns illuminated paths all throughout St. James, the lights in this part of the cemetery had been strangely extinguished. Dio took special care to avoid tripping over potted flowers, wreaths, and low grave markers.

As he moved closer to the source of the sound and the voice became clearer, he realized that it was not singing but weeping. Weeping, in such a heartrending and delicate way that, at a distance, this flow of tears sounded like a sweet and somber melody.

In the middle of a clearing where no trees stood, Dio spotted a shadow on the most ornate memorial in the cemetery.

A marble angel stood eight feet tall, its wings spread wide. The white stone gleaming in the moonlight would have made a picturesque scene, were it not for the black spot that obscured most of its chest.

Within the outstretched arms of the angel was the shadow—a wiggling, moving, weeping bit of space that seemed darker than dark itself, as though a black hole had opened in the middle of the cemetery. That is, if black holes were tiny sobbing things that writhed about uncomfortably in the arms of a marble angel.

"Erebus...is that you?" Dio said softly. He could sense that no one else was in the graveyard, yet it felt somehow inappropriate to speak at a regular volume.

The weeping stuttered and stopped. There was a sniffling sound, then the shadow extended and turned. *Something* took notice of Dio.

Slowly, the shadow oozed and dropped from the arms of the angel and approached Dio, taking on a more recognizable form as it moved—a child, a boy, maybe seven or eight years old, with shaggy hair and big eyes, red-rimmed and damp.

"Dionysus?" asked the small voice, still cracking and trembling with unspeakable grief. "Wh-what are you doing here?"

Dio squinted in the darkness. He took a step to the side to better examine the child in the moonlight.

"So, it is you, Erebus? But why are you a little kid?"

Dio had seen Erebus before. He often hung around mortal funerals with Thanatos or dined in trendy restaurants with Hypnos—when the latter was awake long enough to enjoy a meal. This was not the way that Erebus normally presented himself. Most times, the personification of darkness looked like nothing more than a cartoon undertaker, tall, thin, and dark. He wore finely tailored black suits and a black, silk top hat. Most of the mortals thought he was a goth or steampunk figure, thanks to his affinity for unique pocket watches and round-rimmed sunglasses. Seldom did anyone imagine they were in the presence of Darkness itself—the very essence of night, distilled into the form of a man.

"Yes, it is I," the child said. "I apologize for my appearance right now. I know it must be confusing. I am merely trying to return my mind and my heart to a time when I was truly happy."

Dio knew that something must have gone terribly wrong. Erebus needed only the cover of darkness to be happy. He was, and always had been, fully and completely at home in the dark. He required nothing more than the absence of light. Darkness was his sustenance and muse, his very lifeblood.

Dio looked around. "Night has fallen, as it always does. Why are you in mourning? You have all you need."

The child was suddenly wrathful. Fresh, hot tears welled in his eyes, and he balled his little fists.

"No, I *had* all that I needed! I had her and she had me! I walked with my beloved night for a thousand years!"

The child threw open his arms and gestured to the world at large, turning in a slow circle, speaking as though he were on stage in a theatre, though Dio was the only one in this audience.

"We worked so well together," Erebus went on, his voice quieter now. "Her power was growing, I knew, but

I was intoxicated by it, I could not see how far she had gone until it was too late. And then, just like that, she cast me aside like I was nothing. Like a plaything with which she had grown bored."

"Who are you talking about?" Dio asked. Then he had an idea, and it astounded him that he had not thought to seek out Erebus first. "Does this have to do with The Darkness?"

Had anyone questioned Erebus about the encroaching doom? Had even Zeus come to him and asked him if he knew what it all meant? After all, if anyone was going to understand what was happening, what was gathering in the mortal night of this world, wouldn't it be Erebus?

With a visible effort, the child managed to calm himself, and then turned his big, watery eyes on Dio.

"I wonder if you even remember her name," he said. "So few do, anymore. That is her doing, you know? She has made both men and gods blind to her works and has attempted to erase her own name from memory."

Dio cocked his head to look upon this child that spoke like someone who had lived a thousand lifetimes. The effect was disturbing.

Erebus continued. "Whenever the others have gone power-mad, they wanted the universe to know it, to cry out their names. But not her. She is too wise, too careful. She has worked in darkness, and she has turned my beautiful darkness against me and against you. Against everything."

The child turned his head to gaze upon the marble angel, and in the white moonlight, Dio saw a thin, red line across his neck. It looked painful, raw, and fresh.

"Erebus, you are clearly very worked up, but you have to help me make sense of this, or I don't know how I will be able to help you," Dio said.

The child released a long breath, a heavy and ancient sigh, as though he were attempting to release all the tension of the ages. He rubbed his neck gingerly; Dio saw that the red line made a full loop around.

"I am beyond help," Erebus said softly. "But someone must try to stop her. If she has gone this far, if she is willing to cast me out of her presence and turn her back on me, then I fear what else she will do."

Dio took the half coin from his pocket. He wondered briefly how Than's rave was going, if the magic had yet worn off. He raised the coin up to the moonlight, holding it between his thumb and forefinger so that Erebus could clearly see it.

"All I need is your half," he said to Erebus. Fear registered in the child's eyes. "I'll tell everyone I stole it from you. Nobody has to know that you've helped me."

Erebus looked from the coin to the dark earth beneath his feet, then again to the marble angel. He considered for a long time before turning back to Dio.

"Take it. I know you'll be able to find your way to the gate, but I cannot guarantee you will make it down there alive."

"And I wouldn't ask you to make such a promise," Dio said.

Erebus produced the other half of the coin. Dio took it and held the two halves together. They glowed slightly, pulsing with a sort of power as their edges aligned; when the light faded, they had fused to form one piece.

A gust of wind blew through the cemetery, and the night turned colder.

At the horizon where the city skyline met the twinkling heavens, stars began to blink out, one by one. It was as if a great, black sheet were being steadily drawn over the earth, swallowing the mortals' cosmos in its folds.

The child looked suddenly uneasy.

"There is one more thing I should tell you," Erebus said, backing away from Dio and toward the marble angel. "I have sensed my daughters nearby. I think they must be following you. I do not have to tell you that is not a good sign."

The three dark vultures that had been circling him all day, Dio thought. Even now, as he looked up to the light of the moon, he could see the black of their wings. Of course, it would be the Keres—airborne spirits of violent death, scavengers that feasted on bloody corpses.

Dio cursed softly, but it also occurred to him that, if he was drawing such dangerous attention, he might be on the right track.

"Thanks for the heads up," he told Erebus as he turned to leave.

As Dio ducked beneath the slouching branches of a weeping willow, hoping to stay concealed from the sky for as long as possible, something fibrous and light brushed against his cheek. He grabbed it, then held it up to the moonlight: a noose, carefully constructed from rough twine. The noose had broken where its loop would have entered the knot.

Dio understood then what had happened to Erebus' neck; as he left the cemetery and slipped into the darkened city streets, he felt pity in his heart.

DIO X ARI III

DIO: Hey...

ARI: Hey.

DIO: I feel like I should apologize to you.

ARI: What for?

DIO: We don't completely understand it ourselves... but a lot of the past, like—our collective past—is missing.

ARI: It's okay.

DIO: I'm serious. I'm sorry Ari.

ARI: I get it, your royal grapehood. I can barely remember someone I met last week. Never mind someone from three thousand years ago.

DIO: It's more than that. When the mortals began to forget, it's like so did we.

ARI: Not like the god of wine and merriment to be so...introspective. Didn't enjoy the party?

DIO: The company could've been better.

ARI: And here I assumed you were always the belle of the ball.

DIO: I met Erebus too.

ARI: I gotta say, if I had to pick what The Darkness is, Erebus seems like a good choice. You know he is literally the deity of darkness, right? I keep telling Hera, but she doesn't listen to me.

DIO: Something was off about him. He was...I don't know, sad. He kept saying that *she* has taken his darkness.

ARI: Who?

DIO: I—don't know. But I'm guessing it wasn't a good breakup.

ARI: If you're about to tell me all this is some of that 'woman scorned' stuff, I'm going to stop you right there—

DIO: What? No. I mean, I don't think so. The Primordials. They're strange. Anarchic, you know? They do things sometimes just because they can. Besides, I'm pretty sure she—whoever she is—broke up with him. And took control of his darkness.

ARI: There's a joke here somewhere about a great divorce lawyer—

DIO: I really wish you wouldn't.

ARI: Once again, my immaculate wit is wasted on the likes of you! Where to next?

DIO: South.

CHAPTER 7

Apollo lay on the couch in the expansive living room of the Mountain View home, somewhere between wakefulness and drunken sleep. It could have been midnight or morning; Apollo had drawn the thick curtains and refused to turn on any lights. The room had an atmosphere of gloom, stale cigarette smoke, and the aroma of self-pity: body odor and boozy breath.

Apollo's cherished guitar sat a few feet away from the sofa, untouched for days. No one had been around. There had been no more surprise visits from Hades, and his last conversation with Dio had been less than pleasant. Apollo was thankful that he still retained enough mystical power that he didn't have to leave the house for food or drink—not that he had been eating much anyway. He mostly swilled wine (or beer, or whatever was near) and smoked cigarette after cigarette, staring blankly at an empty wall until he slipped into a semi-comatose state and did something like sleep for a few hours.

Then came the sound. A deep rumbling, a rhythmic cadence. Faint at first, like something at the edge of a dream. Apollo scarcely stirred. But as the rumbles grew louder, Apollo's eyes flickered open, and he sat up on the couch. He could *feel* the sound in the floor, a subtle vibration that grew as the sound did. An earthquake? In Toronto? It seemed unlikely, but things *were* coming unhinged lately—strange and terrible noises in the night, people missing, holy sites mysteriously vandalized across the city. Perhaps an earthquake wasn't out of the question. Apollo sat with his hands braced on either side of his hips and waited, barely breathing, his eyes straining in the dim light.

The floor in front of him began to open. A square of light appeared as smoothly and as easily as if there had been a trap door there all along. Apollo tensed but did not move from his place on the sofa. He wondered if he was having a drunken hallucination.

The sound was much louder now that the floor gaped—rumble, stop, rumble, stop. Now he could hear another sound, a deep, pained, guttural grunting. It sounded human, and it was getting very close.

Then something blocked the light from the hole in the floor, eclipsing it like a moon in the night sky. Soon, the rounded top of some great and rolling object came into view, like a planet encroaching on the living room.

It was a boulder, massive and almost perfectly round. As it came fully into view, Apollo saw who propelled it and who was making the grunting sounds.

"Sisyphus?"

The man who slowly came into view was dressed only in a pair of black gym shorts. He was ripped with muscle. His arms and legs swelled and twitched as the tendons strained visibly beneath his bronzed and sweating skin. He continued to push the rock ever upward until his entire body was in the living room. Apollo was amazed to see that, rather than rolling out of the hole and resting on the floor of the room, the rock continued its upward trajectory, defying gravity. Apollo realized that this was necessary, all part of Sisyphus' punishment.

Sisyphus paused, bracing the massive weight of the boulder against his shoulder, and turned to look Apollo directly in the face. "Who did you expect?"

Apollo stared back a moment before he replied, "I wasn't expecting anyone, really."

Sisyphus nodded slowly, knowingly. He inspected the palms of his calloused hands.

"You have been hiding in here while the world around you cries out in distress," he said.

Apollo rose to his feet, unsteady, but determined. "You don't understand," he said. "I have done a terrible thing. I cannot show my face, I cannot take it back. I am a shame and a traitor. I should be cast into the deepest pits of Tartarus."

Sisyphus grunted, something like a smirk on his weathered face.

"Apollo," he said. "Do you know what is more fruitless than pushing a rock up a hill for eternity?"

Apollo made no answer but cocked his head and waited.

"Wallowing in self-pity," Sisyphus continued. "When you hide from your mistakes, from your problems, you benefit no one. Most times, you only succeed in making the situation much, much worse. I am here because the old gods sent me. They believed that I might have something to say about eternal regret, and they seemed to think you needed to hear it."

Sisyphus raised his face and sniffed at the air. He looked around, seeming to see the room for the first time. He struggled to conceal a look of disgust.

"Perhaps," he said, "you would like to roll this stone, and I could go out and try to make things right in the world. What do you think?"

Sisyphus raised an eyebrow. Apollo knew that he was being facetious. No one could take Sisyphus' burden, no one could roll that stone besides him; it was irreversible.

"But I have made such a terrible mess of things," Apollo said. "I have betrayed my father, and—"

Apollo choked on his own words, unable to continue. When he looked up again, Sisyphus' expression had softened. His dark eyes looked deeply into

Apollo, through him and to the place where he held his darkest guilt and deepest regret.

"Your solitude feeds your pain," Sisyphus said. "The only remedy for your grief is action—*meaningful* action. Do not get stuck behind a rock on a steep hill. Take it from the one who has pushed that rock for eternity: nothing can change until you do."

With that, he turned his body carefully back toward the boulder, resetting the weight against the front of his shoulder and the palms of his hands. With a great, straining grunt, he set the rock moving again, up, up, and up. A space opened in the high ceiling of the room, corresponding with the one that was now closing in the floor. Sisyphus continued to defy physics, climbing the invisible hill until nothing showed but his legs, then his feet. And then he was gone, and the room was just as it had been before: dark and dismal.

Apollo took a deep breath and rubbed his stubbled face with both hands. His fingers came away damp, his face wet with tears. He then walked to the great, floor-to-ceiling windows that comprised one wall of the room and wrenched the curtains open.

※

WHILE THE LOCATION OF THE ENTRANCE TO THE Underworld is technically a secret, it is also not really a secret at all—at least not for the gods. If anyone truly desires in their heart to walk through those gates, the entrance will reveal itself to them.

It was with this feeling that Dio travelled through the night. The stars were all but gone, and inky darkness seemed to flow through the city streets like flood waters. Yet, every turn that Dio took felt like the right one, for death and despair pulled at him like a cord attached to his chest, drawing him onward, deeper into the unnatural night.

It was too dark to see the black shapes of the three Keres as they circled above, but he was ever aware of them: their foul and evil presence simply could not be ignored. They were waiting, anticipating the moment of his death, and then they would feed. He truly hoped to deny them their meal tonight.

Finally, he found himself in the financial district, on streets abandoned save for the occasional homeless person shuffling along the sidewalks looking for a safe place to bed down for the remainder of the night.

Dio had been walking among the tall buildings for a while when he realized that he was being followed by one of the huddled and disheveled figures. He might not have noticed, but the poor soul pushed a shopping cart with a squeaky wheel, and the sound echoed in the empty street.

He stopped and waited as the figure approached, one hand on the switchblade in his coat pocket. Dio knew that most of these unfortunate souls were harmless, and a few were even forgotten gods, but there was always the chance of a madman rambling in the night, and he was not about to be caught off-guard. Not for a second time.

As the person drew near, however, he released his grip on the knife, sensing something familiar in the jerky movements.

"You seek what seeks you. How convenient!" the female voice crooned as she drew near to Dio.

"Aunt Ino?"

She drew back her hood and showed her face. Ino was as beautiful as she was mad. Dio had not seen her in years. Her hair was long, greying, and tangled, her face creased and browned by the elements, but her green eyes still shone like emeralds, and her smile was kind.

"Young Dionysus, you always tramp in the night," she said. "Watch out, lest you be trampled!"

She laughed and Dio chuckled along with her, yet he knew better than to disregard anything she said. Aunt Ino was crazy, but she spoke wisdom in her own way.

"Aunt Ino," Dio said, getting serious. "Do you have any word of my father? Is Zeus all right? Am I doing the right thing?"

It was a lot to ask at once, and Dio felt a little embarrassed, but Ino was unfazed, as though she had been expecting precisely these questions.

"Ah, the King of the Gods fell victim to his petulant child. He is chained by shadows in the nether wild. You'll get there soon and see for yourself. But take this gift. Protect yourself."

Ino reached into the collection of bags and dirty parcels that filled her shopping cart, rummaging around for something. Presently, she produced a package of baloney and placed it in Dio's hand. Dio furrowed his brow as he inspected the package. Somehow it was still cold, as if it had just been pulled from the refrigerator.

"Um...thank you?" he said, but Ino was already walking away, pushing her noisy cart and humming a tune that Dio thought he recognized from another lifetime.

He continued down the street in the direction he felt drawn. He almost stopped at a trash can to dispose of the baloney but thought better of it. Those who ignored Ino's cryptic warnings and bizarre blessings often regretted it.

Soon, the towering facade of the Day Gone Capital building rose before him, the upper floors disappearing into the high darkness. Something twisted deep in his gut, and he knew that the entrance was near, just ahead, at the base of the building. Dio circled around to an alleyway and found his suspicions to be correct. There was a red door at the back of the building, unmarked, inauspicious, but crackling with magical intensity.

He entered the alley with a cautious gait, glancing over his shoulder to make sure he wasn't being tailed by some unsuspecting mortal that was about to get the surprise of their life. He could hear the Keres in the sky above him as they began to call out to one another; they expected their meal would be coming soon.

As Dio neared the door, there was a sudden roll of thunder that doubled and then tripled, the sound overlapping itself, an electrical storm in full stereo. But no, not thunder, there was no storm. The source of the rumbling soon flickered into existence in the space between Dio and the door. It growled and snarled with the sound of the heavens crashing down into the mountains.

Cerberus. The three-headed dog of the Underworld.

Cerberus pawed the ground, claws scrabbling the earth with a sound like rending steel. All three heads showed long, dagger-like teeth, dripping with acidic drool. Six eyes glowed yellow in the dark of the alleyway, malice and fury unrestrained in its gaze.

The Keres cheered with the guttural sounds of vultures on a carcass.

Dio stood motionless. He was continually drawn toward the red door, but he was blocked by the massive bulk and deadly jaws of Cerberus.

Then Dio felt the weight of the baloney in his pocket, and he nearly laughed out loud. He slowly reached into his coat and removed the red and yellow package that Aunt Ino had gifted him just moments earlier. *Trust Aunt Ino to know how to tame the hounds of hell. And then neglect to tell me.*

Cerberus ceased his snarling and turned his three heads to the side, all ears on point. Dio opened the package and divided the processed meat into three even portions as the Keres hissed overhead. One by one, he fed the heads of Cerberus, tossing the meat into the air where they caught it with ease and swallowed it without seeming to chew at all. When all had been fed, the demon dog wagged its tail and crouched down before him. He reached out and scratched one head behind the ear, and with his other hand, rubbed another under the chin. The third head whined piteously and nuzzled his shoulder with a massive, wet nose. Soon, all three tongues were lapping at him. Three times the kisses.

The red door behind Cerberus opened on its own, and the dog seemed content to let a damp Dio pass, but there then came a hideous chorus of screeches from the dark sky. The awful calls echoed off the close buildings in the alleyway and caused Cerberus to whip all three heads skyward, snarling and scanning the darkness.

Furious, the Keres descended all at once. In the meager light, Dio could see that they no longer resembled mere vultures, but now showed their grotesquely human faces, their sharp teeth and blazing eyes. Black wings sprouted from their grey, naked backs, and their nails were long and black as talons.

The Keres converged on Dio from three directions, screaming for his blood as they dropped from the sky like bolts of lightning. He fell to the ground and braced for a collision, knowing he couldn't make it to the door before the first one reached him. Just as he was sure he would be feeling teeth in his neck or talons in his back, there was a mighty growl that drowned out the cries of the Keres. The first vulture-woman was slapped from the air by the deadly paw of Cerberus, and he caught the next in his jaws as easily as if she had been a tennis ball tossed in a game of catch.

Cerberus bit down, the sound of crunching bone audible above the shrieks of the other two sisters—one of which lay sprawled on the ground where she had been swatted. Cerberus shook his head back and forth, the body of his prey flailing limply. He released the body, and it crumpled to the earth between his front feet.

Dio scrambled back against the wall as the other two sisters resumed their attack, now focusing on the gatekeeper to the Underworld. Dio vaguely thought he might be able to use the distraction to make a run for the door, but he was entranced by the battle between these deadly legends of the Underworld.

The beast that Cerberus had first swatted soon found herself again beneath his paw, and this time he held her fast to the ground as he snapped at the third Kere, who was flying frantically about his three heads, slashing at his ears with her long, black claws.

Soon, she flew too near and was caught in one of his unforgiving jaws. Cerberus wasted no time in toying with her. He bit her into two pieces and tossed her aside before turning his attention to the final sister, crushing her under his huge paw.

There was silence and the smell of blood, and the macabre rain of black feathers continued to fall around Dio and his new canine friend. Cerberus sniffed the air, scanned the darkness above, and seemingly satisfied that the danger had passed, wagged his tail and gave Dio another lick with what Dio decided was the most affectionate of the three heads.

With that, the dog stepped aside. As soon as Dio entered the doorway and gazed down into the depthless darkness below, accessible via a lavish, green-carpeted stairway at his feet, the door closed silently behind him.

Dio began his slow descent into the Underworld, content in the knowledge that Cerberus had his back.

CHAPTER 8

Green. Green. Winding ever downward into dark and danger.

Dio felt as though he had been walking down the green-carpeted stairs for hours. Fatigue set in. How long had it been since he had slept? Since he had eaten? He shook the thoughts out of his head. It didn't matter now. There was no time to rest.

He was vaguely aware that the carpet beneath his feet gradually turned to moss, and the perfectly uniform granite stairs transformed into rough stone, uneven and treacherous. Glimmering eyes blinked at him from the surrounding darkness; there was a hissing and skittering as larger things devoured smaller things.

The subterranean basement feel from the top of the steps was gone. There was open space now, and breezes that were neither cool nor refreshing. Electricity in the air.

Tartarus. The Underworld. Realm of Hades...and what else?

When the ground beneath his feet at last leveled out, he found himself on a great plain. It was impossible to tell how expansive the space was because everything was draped in shadows that seemed to be alive, moving of their own volition. The landscape constantly shifted, obscuring any clear perception of what was what. There was murky light from an unknown source—no sun in the sky, no moon, no stars. The illumination filtered through a layer of grey-brown clouds that defined the atmosphere in every direction.

When he turned to look, the stairway was gone, as though it had receded, returned itself back into the natural bleak neutrality of the scene.

Dio chose a direction at random and began to walk, wrapping his jacket tightly around his shoulders as a sudden gust tore at him. These dusty winds soon revealed themselves to be an entity in themselves, brief and violent, seemingly coming from every direction at once, biting at his ears with whispered words.

Motherless.
Fatherless.
Purposeless.

It was as though Dio were being herded by cold nature itself, though he suspected that, down here, nothing was truly natural, and that if he allowed the winds to dictate his direction of travel, he would soon be hopelessly lost. In more ways than one.

In fighting the elements, Dio found himself turned around. What was he looking for, and where should he expect to find it? He closed his eyes and willed himself to feel the presence of the King of the Gods, and then was somewhat shocked to realize that he was not thinking of "Zeus" but rather, his mind reached out for "Father."

Something brushed against his leg and he jumped, hands raised defensively, prepared to fight tooth and nail with whatever strange beasts the Underworld might boast.

But what had touched him was neither beast nor god nor mortal. Dio wasn't sure what it was.

The object was orb-like in shape and tumultuous in aspect. It was like a storm of ash trapped within a glass ball, but there was no glass. When it touched Dio, there was a soft strafing of his pant leg, a gentle tug, a feeling of warmth and familiarity, a sensation made even stranger by the bleak and foreign terrain that stretched out forever on all sides.

The orb bumped against him a couple more times and then began to move away before pausing, as though waiting for him to follow. Being altogether lost, alone and uncertain about his direction, Dio acquiesced and began to trail the object, which he had already decided was a life force, through the slate plain of the Underworld. At times, the orb moved far enough ahead that the blowing dust obscured it, but Dio realized that the ashy surface of the ball emitted its own soft light, warm and yellow from within, as though the maelstrom of ash were enveloping a miniature sun at its core.

The orb cut a straight and certain path. It did not roll, but rather hovered just off the ground, untroubled by the jagged surfaces and loose stones that slowed Dio in his pursuit. Dio began to hear water rushing, and the winds calmed. A dense mist, a wall of vapor, emanated from a crevasse in the land. From where the mist terminated abruptly jutted the prow of a wooden boat.

As Dio and the orb approached, a familiar figure stepped forth from the fog. Charlie looked much the same as he had when he piloted his ferry across the Don, but his attire had changed. He now wore the long, dark robes of lore, and a broad-brimmed hat hid his eyes.

"Aren't you going to ask, 'Where to?'" Dio joked.

Charon seemed to be staring down at the ball of ash, though it was impossible to tell where his gaze actually fell.

"There is only one destination down here, Dionysus," he replied.

Very well, no jokes then, Dio thought as he stepped aboard the boat. The orb hovered along as Charon pushed off, and the wooden ferry bobbed and rocked into the interminable and unknowable currents of the Styx.

THE OTHER SIDE OF THE RIVER WAS DOMINATED BY A different weather system altogether. There were no winds; in fact, the air didn't move at all. It was far hotter, creating a suffocating blanket of humidity that hung oppressively over the land.

Moans and wails, the laughter and shouts of the dead, echoed off stone cliffs and through petrified forests. There was a clear path now—only one—and it led directly toward a horizon of flickering purple that seemed less like illumination and more like a different kind of darkness, a darkness suffused with power and energy and malice. Dio did not need to watch the progress of his guide orb to know that this was where he would begin to find answers to his questions.

As he walked, he began to speak to the orb, and while the being did not make any audible reply, he could not help but sense that it was listening to him with keen interest.

"I am looking for my father—Zeus, King of the Gods," he said. "He has been missing for some time. I don't know if he is here, but I'm sure that this place has something to do with his disappearance...and with The Darkness."

The orb pulsed in odd patterns, as though it were trying to speak to Dio through some language he could not decipher. But it was good to have a companion in such an unsettling realm, and he found himself confiding more in the orb.

Dio continued. "I should have listened to my father.

He knew something was coming, but now it may be too late. The mortals are in danger and the pantheon is depleted. Most of us act more like mortals than anything else. Sorry, you probably don't understand the world up there. You're lucky."

At that, the globe began to burn brightly, the light within suffusing the swirling ash and causing the entire globe to glow with such radiance that Dio had to shade his eyes. There was a ringing, like a thousand tiny chimes, but he could not tell if the sound was real or if it was just a failure of his senses. When the light and sound finally faded, he was standing before a sheer rock face that towered so far into the sky that he could not discern its reaches. Bolts of lightning streaked down the face of the cliff and struck the ground all around, blackening the earth and sending showers of sparks and tiny bits of stone flying. Other bolts ran horizontal across the rock wall, tracing seemingly impossible lines from left to right and back again. The entire effect was of a grid of smoldering electricity, alive and crackling across a massive geological artifice. At the center of this grid was a square of space where no lightning travelled, a plot of near darkness in the midst of the blinding spectacle.

Through squinting and burning eyes, Dio saw his father in the middle of that blank space, manacled brutally and securely to the face of the cliff, high above the ground.

As Dio watched, Zeus was repeatedly trying to

cast his own lightning down or out into the space around him, to create chaos or a reaction that might free him, but his bolts were always intercepted and absorbed by the foreign streaks of electricity that imprisoned him.

"Zeus!" Dio screamed. Then, after no reaction: "Father!"

The chest of Zeus ceased heaving, and he relaxed in his manacles. Somehow, the words had penetrated the noise and tumult of the electrical storm. The lightning still struck and crashed, breaking sections of rock loose from the sheer face of the cliff. But Zeus stared down at his son as though he were seeing him for the first time. He beamed with genuine glee.

"Dionysus, my boy!" he boomed over the crackling and crashing lightning. "You have come to me! What, pray tell, have your guides told you?"

Dio froze in place. It would not be peculiar to balk at such a question, but Dio was curious because his father was less interested in how Dio had found him and more interested in what he may have learned along the way.

Was this all a ploy? Was his father even truly captive, or had he positioned himself as bait to allow Dio to be pathetic prey, gods forbid?

Dio stared up into the lightning-streaked sky. "Why?"

Zeus beamed, despite the assault he was undergoing, and a strange smile curled one side of his mouth.

"Because I have waited for you to come and save me since before I needed saving!"

This was not what Dio had expected.

"Do you feel better now, having met your mother?" Zeus called down.

"She gave me a place to sleep and some advice. I suppose that was helpful," Dio called back.

"Not Hera, boy!" Zeus shouted, a peculiar grin on his bearded face, "I am talking about Semele, your mother, right next to you!"

Dio looked around, turning in cautious circles to make certain that he saw everything that might be going on around him. Finally, his gaze settled on the glowing orb of tumultuous ash that had remained his beacon through the grim landscape.

"Mother?" he asked, and the light glowed warmer. "Mother? Is it you? Are you in there?"

With each question that Dio asked, the orb pulsed and shone.

"How is this possible?" he asked, kneeling closer to the orb.

Slowly and with trembling hands, Dio reached toward the orb, his eyes transfixed by the swirling storm of ash and light contained within. When he placed his hands on the surface that was not really a surface, his mind was suddenly flooded with a vibration. It was a sensation of frequency, of sound as much as feeling.

A voice. Her voice, the voice that he had never

heard but still would have recognized with his heart a galaxy away.

"My Dionysus," she said in his mind. "I have waited so very long to be with you. I am so happy that you have come."

Tears welled in Dio's eyes as he continued to touch the orb before him, gazing into it as though it might hold all the secrets of the universe—and indeed it might.

"Mother."

It was not a question, but a statement of both awe and relief, an unburdening of the soul and the quenching of the awful fire that had always burned so deeply within him.

"How?" he asked.

The light within the orb flickered with a rapid intensity. The voice in his head sighed.

"It is not easily explained," she said, her voice like running water, like birdsong, like a breeze through the cedars of Athens. "But I have come to understand some things about dark magic in all my years here, so I will tell you what I can. Sometimes, when a mortal dies in moments of extreme emotion, something powerful occurs. Usually, this means very little in the physical world, perhaps a thunderstorm or a crashing wave, little things of which mortals take no notice. However, if there is an entity close by that has the knowledge and the skill to harness that power at the moment of death, and to preserve it...then there is a greater danger."

Dio wrinkled his brow with concentration. He looked at his mother and then at Zeus. His father was scarcely visible within the grid of electricity, but Dio was certain that he could see a look of grief and duress upon Zeus' face as he gazed at the scene unfolding below him. There was no way that Zeus could hear the words that Semele was speaking into Dio's mind, yet he seemed to understand exactly what was being revealed.

"So," Dio ventured, "are you saying that your pain, your essence, has been trapped within this sphere for millennia? That you have been used to power some sort of upheaval from the Underworld? Mother...are you... The Darkness?"

As Dio uttered the words, there was a drastic shift in the air. The lightning that contained Zeus sputtered and shrieked, and the purple sky darkened to an inky black. The change was more than something Dio could see and hear—he could feel it closing in, suffocating him. He suddenly felt as though he were wrapped tightly in thick blankets that weighed down his limbs and stifled his breath.

"Not precisely," his mother said, her voice more urgent now, somewhat hushed, as though she were trying to explain everything before someone else arrived. "I am not *she,* I am not The Darkness—but The Darkness cannot exist without me. Do you understand? I am like a...what's the word...an *engine*. Without me, she is still evil, she is still darkness, but she cannot *go* anywhere. But with me, and once everything is prepared, she will be able to go *everywhere*."

Dio shook his head, trying to clear the cobwebs of fear and confusion that wrapped around his consciousness. He struggled to articulate a plan of action. He wished there were living things here, anything: grass, a tree, wildflowers. He could draw energy and peace from these things, they were symbiotic with him, and...that was it!

"Mother, I have to take you away from this place! Once you are far from this Darkness, *she* will be weakened. After that, I will return with my brother Apollo to defeat this evil and free Father!"

The light within his mother's orb softened and turned a dark amber. Dio couldn't tell if it was something she did, some indicator of a change in emotion, or if the encroaching darkness made everything else dim.

"It's not that simple, Dio," she said, her voice now barely audible over the droning and grinding sounds that came from everywhere, from within and without. "I am bound to her. There is no way to remove me from her vicinity, not for mortals and not for gods. But there is one thing you can do that may weaken her for long enough that you and my beloved Zeus might escape the Underworld. You can destroy me."

Dio felt as though he had been stabbed through the chest. He nearly dropped the form that was his mother as he staggered back.

"Destroy you? No! I have only just found you! I will not! *Can*not! There has to be another way!"

A warmth moved into his hands and up his arms. It was a sweet and comforting feeling, so incongruous with the chaos and fear that was raging all around him. He recognized it somehow as a phenomenon he had never truly experienced. It was the warmth of a mother's embrace.

"Dio, she is too strong," she said. "She is nearly strong enough to free herself, to unleash herself on the mortals, I can feel it! If you will not do what I ask, then you must flee, right now, or you and your father will both be erased from memory. You have fallen into her trap, and others will as well. Once the pantheon is sufficiently forgotten, she will rule the earth."

"*Who? Who* will rule the earth? I need to know this enemy who has taken both my mother and my father!"

Suddenly, he was being dragged, or pushed, he could not tell which. He could not be certain which one of his parents was doing it, but he was being propelled with the insistent love of a mother or father. His feet scrabbled on the rocky earth. The winds tugged at his clothing and mussed his hair. Through his tousled bangs, he could see the glowing orb of his mother, now white with inner light, as though she were a beacon, a lighthouse to guide his eventual return. High above, Zeus remained pinned helplessly to the crackling cliff, but now with a look of pleasure on his face.

You called me Father.

As Dio was carried over the river Styx—not by ferry, but by the magical goodness of two loving parents—he heard Zeus' voice boom and carry over the vast expanses of the Underworld as he greeted The Darkness that had arrived and fell upon them.

"Hello, Nyx. You old bitch."

CHAPTER 9

What was it she had said? The voice from the storm of ash, the glowing orb of maternal warmth—his mother, Semele. *"We are connected..."* But not he and her, not mother and son, but Semele and...The Darkness.

Darkness.

Dio found himself in perfect darkness. It was perfect in that he could still see. Utter darkness would have been imperfect, because it would have meant that he did not escape the terror and the indecipherable evil that was closing in on him when his mother bade him farewell and forcibly propelled him from the Underworld. The last thing he remembered was the skittering of loose stones and the stink of the infernal mist as he rocketed over the River Styx. He must have blacked out.

But now he no longer sensed that death and hopelessness. This darkness was punctuated—no, striated—with bars of dim, blue light. The bars were before his eyes and on his hands and arms, arms which were wrapped tightly around his bent knees. He sensed that he sat on a floor and that something fuzzy was tickling the top of his head. He reached up and felt fur, whiskers...and teeth.

Dio shouted and tried to scramble away, but he was trapped in a very small space with something fanged and feral. He kicked against his tiny prison, hearing his own shouts roar in his head as his hands and feet banged and thumped against walls closing in from all directions. Suddenly, the barred wall swung open, and a lean figure stood over him, silhouetted in pulsing blue light.

"You better quiet down before the manager kicks us out," demanded a familiar voice.

Dio went quiet and blinked at the figure in front of him, his eyes adjusting. Her features came into focus.

"Ari?"

Ari stood with her hip cocked and one hand on her waist, looking down on him with some mixture of disdain and concern. Behind her, a television squalled with the laugh track of a popular sitcom, creating the blue and shifting light in the otherwise darkened room.

"Wh-where are we?" Dio managed. He felt equally confused and embarrassed to be in such a position and to not recall how he found himself in it.

"Jacktown Motel," Ari said matter-of-factly. "It's not

the Ritz, but I didn't think I should drag you back to Hera's again. Not the way you were carrying on."

Dio began to crawl out of the closet. Suddenly, he remembered the toothy beast that had been lurking behind him and he spun on his knees to see what might emerge from the dark depths. Ari reached past him and flipped on the closet light. A limp and somewhat bedraggled mammal hung, dead-eyed, from a wooden hanger.

"It's a faux fox stole," Ari said. "Sorry, I didn't know you wanted to be alone in there."

"D-did you keep me in a closet?!"

"Of course I did, handsome. That's where I keep all my precious things. Like my very authentic fox stole."

※

ONCE DIO HAD SETTLED SHAKILY ONTO THE MOTEL room bed and she had given him a plastic cup of tap water, Ari explained that she had gone out to find him. Hera had received word, through her usual channels, of the Keres being attacked and devoured in an alleyway. Suspecting that the massacre might have something to do with Dio's mission, Ari had set out to examine the scene, but had encountered him some blocks away, shuffling and rambling, in a fugue state, senseless as a drunk.

"You just kept mumbling about your mother and father…and then you said a name that I had nearly forgotten. In fact, I had forgotten it, until you said it. You kept saying—"

"Nyx," Dio interrupted, finally feeling steady again. "I said Nyx, didn't I?"

Ari looked shaken. It was not an expression that Dio could have imagined on her. To him, she seemed completely unflappable, aloof, tough as nails.

"Yes," she said. "Is that who this is all about? Is she... is she real?"

Dio said nothing, but he could tell that the look on his face when he met Ari's eyes was enough to get the truth across.

Ari slowly settled into a stained and dated accent chair.

"I thought she was just some old legend," she said.

Dio rose and walked to the dresser, over which hung a large mirror. His clothes were filthy and wrinkled. His hair hung in greasy tentacles about his face. There were circles under his eyes that were too dark to cover, even with concealer.

"Ari," he finally said. "We are all nothing more than legends. But that doesn't make us any less dangerous."

He turned and looked down on her. She looked up at him with hope in her eyes. It energized him. Something was coming together in his mind; he was able to feel the wisdom of ages, the mystical and forbidden secrets that had become faded with time and mottled with wine. Dio saw elements coming together to work as a cohesive unit. It was as though he were manning a post on the moon and watching all the happenings here on earth, able to see from above how The Darkness moved and why, and what might be done to stop the steady advance of that lurking malevolence.

"I think I have a plan," he told Ari. "But I'm going to need some help."

Ari's expression changed. She transformed back into the bored and confident woman he had met in the greenhouse at Hera's and doubtlessly other times before, those fragments still hidden somewhere in his ancient mind. He could feel them, but not quite remember why he felt such things. Such is the way with the gods in today's world.

"I'm sitting right in front of you," she said. "Why don't you stop being so dramatic and just tell me what you've got in mind?"

※

ARI WAS AT THE SMALL DESK, BANGING AWAY AT HER laptop, sending yet another email. Dio paced back and forth between the kitchenette and the motel bathroom, sighing into his phone, hanging up, punching out quick texts, dialing numbers.

He spoke into the phone. "They are forgetting us, that is the key, Athena...I know what you call yourself *now,* but that is the point of all this, we need to let the mortals believe again...yes, yes, something like that would do. Every little thing helps. Thank you!"

He felt like he was hosting a telethon, a staged contrivance to raise awareness of the gods of the pantheon. Ari was his unwitting cohost, and everyone else was a viewer or a listener somewhere out there in fantasy land—but it was a fantasy land where the most important fantasies no longer mattered.

"Remembrance!" he had told Ari. "That is our best weapon."

Nyx had slowly risen to power in the Underworld as mortal remembrance of the gods had faded. He could feel it now, triggered by the words of his mother. He didn't quite understand how Nyx had subjugated Hades, who had always been such a stickler when it came to his place of power, but those details didn't matter now. All that mattered was making the people remember—and believe. Dio was sure that if the mortals of Toronto would again place their faith in the pantheon, he and his kin would have the power to defeat Nyx, Hades, and whoever else had signed on to do their bidding.

"I've got Aphrodite on board!" Ari reported. "And is she ever prompt. Just look at this tweet!"

Ari leaned over so that Dio could see her laptop screen. It showed a Twitter post of an old photo: Aphrodite and Zeus. Both were smiling affectionately, because, hey, it was Aphrodite! Dio saw that his father was wearing his red baseball cap and sleeveless flannel. The shot must have been taken from sometime in the 1990s. A caption beneath the photo read, "#TBT to me with the ORIGINAL stud! #onceagodalwaysagod."

"Good work," Dio said. "She has more followers than Bono, that should help to get things trending. I just got off the phone with Athena. She was reluctant at first, doesn't want to make waves and lose her shot at tenure, but I think I wore her down. She said she would put together a website that breaks down the stories—*our* stories—into a kid's cartoon."

"Get 'em young," Ari replied, raising a hand for a high five, which Dio obliged. "I've sent an email to Hestia. She could pull some serious awareness with her homemaking program."

Dio looked up from his phone. Still no reply from Apollo.

"Hestia has a show?"

Ari spun in the desk chair and gave him a shocked look, her eyebrows raised gracefully.

"Um...yeah," she said. "She does cooking segments with that famous rapper."

Dio's jaw dropped. "Wait—Hestia is—"

"Hell yeah she is!" Ari cut in.

"I didn't even recognize her!"

"She looks great, right?"

Still pondering this latest revelation, Dio dialed Apollo again.

"You have reached Apollo. I am either too deep in creative ecstasy to answer your call, or—"

Dio hung up, unable to suffer through his brother's outgoing message one more time.

"I need to go to my house," he told Ari. "Clearly you

have better connections than me. Would you mind reaching out to anyone else you can think of?"

Ari didn't turn her eyes away from her computer screen, though a part of him wished that she would look at him once more before he left.

※

THE HOUSE ON MOUNTAIN VIEW WAS DARK, SAVE FOR one window on the second floor. Apollo's room.

Dio flicked on the light switch at the bottom of the staircase and mounted the stairs two at a time, calling his brother's name. He hurried down the long hallway at the top of the staircase, now muttering under his breath.

"A time like this and my brother, the hero, can't be troubled to leave his den. Leave it to nasty, brooding, unpredictable Dionysus to save the day. Ridiculous—"

Dio stopped mid-stride, shocked that he had just referenced himself by his ancient name. He had long since ceased to think of himself as Dionysus, god of wine and revelry. It had been much easier—and more fun—to just be Dio, party god. However, the circumstances and experiences of the past couple of days had changed him. Something had shifted within. A part of his ancient soul returned to dignity and divinity. He had to admit that it felt good. Becoming and believing himself to be an entity of power and esteem made him feel stronger, more confident in the face of the dire enemy which they now faced.

He started forward again, striding toward the faintly glowing rectangle of light that was Apollo's doorway. Dio found the door unlocked and burst in without knocking.

"Would it kill you to pick up your phone, you muscle-bound—"

The room was empty, brightly lit, and quite frankly a mess. It was unlike Apollo to not keep his belongings in neat order, but right now his room looked more like Dio's. Clothes and books were scattered everywhere. Empty liquor and beer bottles cluttered the flat surfaces, and the room contained the fetid stench of stale cigarette smoke. Dio moved to open a window and allow some fresh air to dispel the general sourness of the room.

As he lifted the sash, he caught a glimpse of a vague shadow on the lane that led up to the house. It was anthropomorphic and moved quickly, the shape of a man with a guitar strapped to his back.

Dio turned and scanned the ruined room. Ebony, Apollo's prized Stratocaster, sat on her stand in the one clean corner of the room. Next to Ebony was another, empty stand, the one that usually held Apollo's acoustic guitar.

❧

IN THE MEAGER LIGHT OF A STREETLAMP, APOLLO checked his watch. It was after five in the morning. He looked to the east and scowled. The low horizon should be gradually turning purple by now, heralding the coming sunrise, but this morning there was only blackness. The sky looked as though it were midnight rather than nearly dawn. Something was wrong, and Apollo knew it had to do with what had been troubling his father.

He had cut through the park at the edge of the suburb, keeping to the shadows of the trees, not wanting to be seen by man or beast as he followed the pull of his heart, which guided him ever onward toward the city. The words of Sisyphus echoed in his ears. He set his jaw and steeled his resolve against the grief and guilt that threatened to overcome him with every step.

It was good to be out of the house. The gentle breeze swept the cobwebs of self-loathing and intoxication out of his head. He was beginning to feel like himself again, and he knew that action was necessary. He could no longer sit idly by while the fruits of his betrayal played out across the land of mortals.

As he crossed the tree line of the park, he cast one last look over his shoulder at the Mountain View home. The only light in the house shone from the window of his own bedroom. In that window he saw the outline of a thin and angular man. His half-brother Dio.

What had Dio discovered in these past days, and what must he think of Apollo now?

There was no time for these thoughts, Apollo knew, for he had a date with destiny somewhere in the guts of the city. He would move through darkness and shadows and curse the day that failed to come, but he would not stop, and he would not be overcome by his own doubts and grief. Apollo reached back and patted the acoustic guitar that swung gracefully against his muscled back.

"Stay by me, Jolene, and we will try to make the world a more beautiful place."

Deep in the Underworld, Zeus hung against the rock cliff face, his muscles relaxed and his face serene. The lightning had ceased not long after Semele expelled Dio from their dark proximity. Zeus had expected as much; the bolts of electricity were more for show than anything. He was familiar with the tactic and had employed it himself over the years, to great effect.

Zeus was still hopelessly bound by the enchanted manacles that held his wrists and ankles to the rock. In another time, another place, he would have wrenched the bindings from the wall as though they were made of paper. But the years had weakened him more than he had realized, and not because of his age, which was of no consequence to him. No, it was the status of his name, his place in the collective memory of the mortal masses, that had weakened him so.

Zeus was bound not by steel, enchanted or otherwise, but by the dismissal of his legend, the failure of the modern scribes to engrave his deeds into the tablets of modern man.

Before him now, the glowing ball of ash and energy that was Semele hovered and hummed and glimmered with light. He gazed into it with an open face and an open mind. They were having a conversation of sorts, an ancient god and his former lover, about the things that they felt happening all around them.

When the lightning stopped, there was a difference in the grim air of the Underworld—an absence. At first, Zeus had thought it was just his body adjusting to the sudden lack of electrical current which had surged all around him, but then Semele communicated to him that she felt it as well. Something had come close and then gone away. They both knew what—or who—it was.

"Nyx has gone to the portal," Zeus said to Semele, who flickered and flashed in agreement. "Even now, she ascends the green stairway to wait at the door. Cerberus will not be able to contain her, if he even tries."

The glowing patterns that Semele emitted were something that Zeus could read as easily as though it were Greek.

"She has gained enough power to enter the world of mortals," she said. "It may be too late to stop her now. Oh, all those poor souls. I cannot bring myself to say what she will do to them, but because I am a part of her, I have been forced to witness terrible things within her imagination. Terrible, unspeakable things..."

The orb began to pulse in a slow and somber way that Zeus knew was Semele weeping. Pictures of her came rushing back to his mind. Details, so acute, that he felt he was falling in love with her for the very first time. He thought of her smell—lavender. He remembered her hair—thick, wavy locks that floated gently in the Grecian breeze. He remembered the smoothness of her skin; the delicate feel of her fingers running through his beard. And he remembered the abundance of love he felt whenever she was near.

"There, there, my sweet Semele," Zeus said, wishing that his arm was free so that he could reach out and touch the essence of this woman so he might bring her comfort in her distress. She had been captive in this place, in this form, for thousands of years; he knew it was in no small part because of him and the pain he had caused her.

"Lest you forget," he said, softly, "gods still roam this land, and when the pantheon is faced with an impossible task, we tend to find ways to emerge victorious."

The orb glowed with what Zeus could only construe as hope.

CHAPTER 10

"Oh, but what of the stories, what of the gods?" Charlie the ferryman sung out, pushing a broken gondola through the mists that shrouded the Don River. "What will become of them? Who can we trust?"

The rusty, trusty, modern ferry remained tied at the dock, its usually noisy and smoking motor quieted. Charon had brought out this relic—something that he had stowed away on the auspices that it had a little more class—when the sun failed to rise that fated morning. Now, with nary a passenger and with pole in hand, he plied the waters and sang in a low, mournful baritone, wondering aloud what might become of the pantheon— and of the world of mortals— now that darkness was upon the land.

From the riverbank, Dio watched the outline of the old boat as it moved aimlessly through the fog, illuminated only by what little light penetrated from the docks and shanties on either side. A part of him wanted to call out to Charon to ask him what he thought of all this. The ferryman's cryptic message from the night prior certainly suggested that he was in possession of at least some sort of privileged information, but the craft was too far offshore. Besides, it was not Charon that Dio was here to see.

In fact, there was no one in particular that he sought at this moment. Rather, he needed to be where the people were. He needed to see if the plans that he and the others had laid during the long night would come to fruition. To see if they would do any good at all.

All along the riverwalk, mortals were moving, most of them paying no attention to the singing ferryman out in the middle of the Don. Some were dressed in suits and dresses, businesspeople off to begin their daily routines. Others were dressed in shorts or sweats, jogging along with earbuds wedged firmly in the sides of their heads, while others walked dogs or carried coffees.

It would have appeared to be an ordinary early morning scene, were it not for the looks of tense concern on the faces of these mortals. Their eyes darted back and forth from the eastern horizon to the cell phones clutched in their hands. Their faces were blue in the unnatural darkness, illuminated only by screens. They ignored their dogs and their agendas and moved about with an absentminded allegiance to routine, all the while preoccupied with one simple, disturbing question: "Why is it so dark?"

Dio wondered what kind of panic and chaos would grip the streets if these mortals could feel what he felt. Yes, they could see the darkness, could understand that something was wrong with the basic functioning of the environment, but if they could they feel The Darkness as Dio felt it, they wouldn't have dared to leave their homes. The air was instilled with a malevolent evil, an insidious vibration that heralded the coming of something unspeakably awful.

He checked his watch and waited for the moment when Athena would launch her new site. He knew it had been a tall order, asking her to have a fully functioning website up and running by morning, but Athena had a battalion of faculty and graduate students at her beck and call, and Dio was confident she would come through.

Just as he thought this, the phone in his jacket pocket chimed and vibrated—the notification for a new email. He checked it. Sure enough, right on time: athenatellsitall.com was live. It was a slick, modern site, well designed and easily navigable. There were tabs for all the major "myths," linked to animated videos where adorable and hilarious characters explained the history of the gods in fast-paced, exciting, and comprehensive skits. Below these videos were links to short presentations on lesser myths; there were even some clever

Easter eggs that pointed to what some of the gods were doing in the modern world.

Even as he was clicking on the new site for the first time, Dio heard other phones beeping and pinging, slowly at first, a scattering of notifications. But, in time, it seemed that most people were scrolling, making small sounds of amusement. Some nodded and chuckled before turning back to the weather, the news, or social media, searching for answers about the unending night. It had been a small wave in a huge pool, but Dio felt a tingle in the dark air. Something fundamental had changed, ever so slightly, as Athena's new site went up and mortals across the city took momentary notice, clicked a few tabs, maybe bookmarked the site for later, and moved on with their own worries and concerns. It wasn't much, but it was enough to make Dio wonder if they just might have a chance after all.

※

At 10 a.m., when the sun still had not made an appearance and fear and unease began to grip the city, some businesses shut their doors and sent their employees home. Other places carried on, trying to act as though nothing were out of the ordinary, but the atmosphere in these offices and grocery stores was tense, quiet, and foreboding. No one knew what to think of the phenomena occurring across the land, and there was little news from abroad. Was it dark everywhere? Did anyone have a theory? Television news reports talked in circles and offered no real answers, so most people changed the channel, looking for something more comforting, a distraction in a dark and uncertain moment.

This is exactly when a special live episode of *Home with Martha* came on—starring Hestia in her modern form: a smart and classy woman, one part supermom and one part boardroom assassin. On this show, she distributed weekly advice about how to remove stains or spruce up garden plants, where to find the best window treatments and how to concoct the perfect lemon soufflé. It was for these latter achievements—her cooking segments—that she was a star. Her cohost on the culinary portion of the show was a popular West Coast rapper from the United States, who had made such a lucrative career out of slinging rhymes that he could now do basically whatever he wished without risking damage to his street credibility. He had chosen to make pastries with Martha.

Now, on the morning that never came, Martha hit the airwaves to serve as a much-needed distraction for countless people across the region. She made slight mention of the odd nature of the day: "Sometimes it gets dark, but we must never lose sight of the light," and then proceeded to introduce the menu for that day's cooking segment. It would be a multi-course meal, a grand and elaborate affair; in fact, she would be dedicating the entire show to it. The theme: Food of the Gods.

"I will be showing you how to make an Aphrodite Ambrosia Salad, Apollonian Shrimp Ceviche, Zeus' Roasted Chicken, and more. For dessert, we will be making Dionysian Wine Tarts." With this, Hestia, as Martha, gave the camera a sly wink.

"As we prepare each dish, I want to tell you the stories behind them; I want to help all of you—my good friends out in TV land—understand the rich and meaningful traditions behind these favorite dishes of mine. Food always tastes best when we know the history behind it, don't you think?"

The screen melted into the *Home with Martha* logo and her theme music filled tens of thousands of living rooms across the darkened city and beyond. Back in the motel, Dio sat on the cheap loveseat, his knee barely touching that of Ari. Their bodies made wild shadows on the wall as the television cast hues and shapes in the otherwise darkened room.

"I feel like..." Ari finally said. "I feel like it might be working."

Dio said nothing at first, only nodding, cautious, as though to be too optimistic might break some kind of spell. He felt it, too, just as he had when Athena launched her site earlier that morning. It was a tingling, but of the spirit rather than the body—like something warm was chipping away at the cold obsidian that hung in the air.

It was the sensation of being remembered. People were beginning to reawaken to the existence of the gods. The curiosity of mortals was being piqued, and the names of the pantheon were once more on their tongues. It was not enough, not yet, but even in that moment, Dio had a vision of the portal to the Underworld. It was trembling and jolting, racked by a furious force from within. There was a black mist that poured out from around the seams of the door, a darkness that was somehow darker than that which covered the land. Nyx was still trapped inside, but she was not giving up.

And neither must we, Dio thought.

※

"I THINK WE HAVE A LITTLE BIT OF A PROBLEM," ARI said.

It was midday, and still the sky outside the motel windows was black as pitch. The local meteorologists had taken to calling it a "bizarre weather event" and insisted that a thick layer of atmospheric disturbance was obscuring the sun. But even these weathermen did not seem to believe their own claims.

"What's up?" Dio asked, coming to lean over Ari's shoulder where she sat before her laptop. They were both exhausted, having not slept in forever, but they had continued to monitor the progress of the gods. Hestia's episode of *Home with Martha* had been nothing short of a miracle. Response on the web had been tremendous, and the recipes—along with their corresponding legends—had already been shared millions of times.

Athena's site was also doing extremely well, as young people, home from school due to the "weather event" flocked to the new animations and plots, latching onto these new characters and adventures—ones that most had never heard before.

Ironically, and much to Dio's surprise, it was Aphrodite's contribution to the cause that was coming up short.

"People just aren't responding well to the Zeus pic," Ari was saying. "And when they do, the response isn't exactly positive. Look at these comments."

Ari scrolled down so that Dio could scan the comment section:

"Get the old guy out of the way, Aphro! I want to see your outfit!"

"Is it Grandparent's Day already?"

"Hey baby, drop the geriatric, and reply to my DM!"

PEOPLE COULD BE SO CRUEL. DIO FOUND HIMSELF feeling quite bad for his father, the King of the Gods. He certainly deserved more respect, but that might have to wait; for now, they needed some creative problem solving.

"I don't get it." Dio said, "It's Aphrodite. She's literally the personification of love and beauty. Why does she receive such ugliness from the mortals?"

Ari gently pushed Dio back with a sigh. "How about you just sit down and look pretty for me? Give that rum-addled raisin in your head a break. I think I know how to handle this one."

Dio stepped back, crossed his arms, and wondered what part of her comment he wanted to reply to first. Ari ignored the perplexed look he was giving her and banged out a quick email to Aphrodite.

IT WAS EARLY AFTERNOON BY THE TIME APOLLO arrived at Yonge-Dundas Square—a commercial and retail hotspot in the city. It was not so much that he had headed there, but it was where his feet took him. There were less people around than normal, which he had expected because of the unexplainable darkness and pressing sense of doom and all, but there was still a decent number of folks milling about. There was even a hotdog vendor, though no one bought his wares, not that he seemed to mind. The old man just stood in place and stared to the east, as though willing the sun to climb into the sky at last.

Apollo found an empty bench and sat down, his

acoustic guitar upon his knee. He was wearing ripped jeans and a black T-shirt, his long hair down and hanging in curls to his shoulders. Apollo lit a cigarette. Especially in the waning light of streetlamps, he looked like nothing so much as a struggling street musician.

The sewer cover a few feet in front of him was belching clouds of steam. As he watched, the steam began to shift and morph, acting in ways that sewer steam should not act. It congealed, solidified, and took form.

Cautiously, moving only his eyes, Apollo glanced around, but no one else in the square seemed to notice the apparition taking shape before him. In moments, the steam darkened to match the surrounding gloom. The only aspect of the anthropomorphic blob that served to identify the entity was a pair of gleaming silver cufflinks.

"Uncle Hades," Apollo said, his tone low. "It's been a minute."

The figure fluttered, coughed, took form again. Now a face was vaguely visible.

"I have been quite occupied, as you might imagine," he said. "Your father sends his regards."

It took every ounce of self-control that Apollo possessed to keep him from lunging at the likeness of his uncle, but he refrained. It would do no good, and he knew it would only serve to make him look mad: a big, shaggy guy with a guitar, attacking a column of sewer steam.

"You can't use my guilt against me anymore," Apollo said. "I've had a change of perspective."

The steam coughed and cackled again. Apollo could tell that Hades was trying to be his usual, arrogant self, but something was off. His uncle was struggling to retain his form; he was in a weakened state, and that gave Apollo a sudden thrill of pleasure that he could barely conceal.

"Ah yes, Sisyphus. I heard he came to pay you a visit, nephew." Hades' voice was full of mocking and malevolence. "Let me tell you, that rock sucker never amounted to anything, so I would take anything he said with a grain of salt."

Across the square, Apollo heard a dozen phones chime. He felt his own phone, silenced and in the pocket of his jeans, vibrate as well. People gazed at their screens; he saw several faces smile as thumbs worked tiny keypads as the mortals posted or reposted according to whatever new social media trend had just begun or ended.

Apollo wondered what might be happening that was enough to distract people from the blanket of darkness that covered the city and—as far as anyone could tell— the world beyond. Suddenly, there was a flickering in the sky. It was something like lightning, yet there were no clouds to be seen (nor were there stars—the sky consisted of a single, solid void of black). The light that illuminated the world for that brief second was not the white, hot light of a summer storm, but a golden glow... the color of sunlight.

As quickly as it began, it ended, and Apollo turned his eyes back to his uncle. Hades was staring into the sky, and he had gone silent.

"What's the matter, Uncle?" he asked. "Things not going quite as planned?"

The black mist swirled over the sewer lid, a whirlpool of wicked intent.

"I may not know what you children are up to," Hades said. "But whatever becomes of the land of mortals, just know you sealed your father's fate when you made a deal with me. There is no miracle you can perform that will break the bonds that hold Zeus in the Underworld. His soul is damned."

Children? He couldn't possibly be referring to...Dio? The god of the sun felt a quiet smile growing within. *Will wonders never cease.*

Apollo twisted a tuning key on his guitar and plucked a string, dialing in a perfect E. Hades cringed at the sound. Encouraged, Apollo began to strum a few cords, slowly and naturally finding his way through the forest of sounds and possibilities, following the path he always took when creating a new song.

"There's a magic in music." Apollo smiled at the swirling hex before him. "A kind that does not expire with the passing of time or the waning of worshipers."

"I AM A...GENIUS!"

Dio jolted awake. He hadn't even realized that he had fallen asleep, but he found himself on the small sofa in the motel room, one cheek wet with his own drool.

Ari was at the desk, her eyes dark and drooping, but full of light. She beamed and pointed at the laptop that still glowed in the darkness behind her.

"Half a million 'likes' already!" she said, practically shouting. Dio pressed a hand to one temple, wishing she would be a little quieter, but still feeling himself joining in her excitement.

"What are you talking about?" Dio croaked.

Ari looked at him as though he were dense.

"Aphro's post," she said. "With the puppy. It's blowing up!"

"Puppy?"

Dio rose and moved to the desk, where the screen showed Aphrodite's Instagram page. The most recent post showed the goddess of love wearing a bright yellow bikini and cuddling a labradoodle puppy with ridiculously huge eyes. The caption read: "Meet Zeus, my new best friend. #ilovezeus."

The counter beneath the photo showed more than five hundred thousand likes.

"How did you know?" Dio asked. "The real Zeus picture was such a disappointing flop. How did you know that this would work?"

Not receiving a reply, Dio turned and walked back to the loveseat, sinking down into its tacky and welcome embrace. He wanted to sleep some more but knew that it would have to wait—time was of the essence, and sleep...well, he'd have plenty of opportunity to sleep if the world were enveloped in endless night.

"Dreams, delusions, and hard-ons," she said finally.

"Pardon?"

"They don't care about her," Ari said. "Her followers. They're only interested in what she can give them. And those three things make the internet go round. Well, those, and videos of men being kicked in the crotch."

Aphrodite had a huge fanbase on social media platforms—one of the largest in the world. If #ilovezeus caught on—along with the social miracles performed by Athena and Hestia—it might put enough affection and awareness of Zeus and the other gods into the hearts of the mortals that Nyx might not be able to break the seal on the portal and enter their world.

It was the *might* that was troubling Dio. What if the mortals' love for the gods was not strong enough to keep The Darkness contained?

CHAPTER 11

Yonge-Dundas Square was slowly beginning to look like its bustling self again. It was still cloaked in darkness, for the sun had yet to return to the horizon. There were flickers now and again, though, golden apparitions that lit the landscape as lightning might, but with a warmer hue.

No, the reason that Yonge-Dundas felt more like a busy city center was because scores of mortals were appearing, moving into the space, drawn by actions and sounds that seemed familiar and provided them respite from their worries, cares, and the stifling gloom they had awoken to.

Apollo stood on the sewer grate, fully enraptured by his song. If he took any notice of the crowd that had grown around him, it did not show. Nor did he acknowledge his accompaniment: a varied and motley cast of street performers and musicians that had gravitated to his rhythms—and had joined in.

There was a violin player with long, swaying dreadlocks, who dipped and droned along, adding a sense of mystery and classical appeal to the tune. An aging rocker had turned up with a battered Gibson Les Paul and a battery-powered Pignose amplifier. He plugged in and had little trouble finding the pocket, Apollo's song was so natural, so inviting. In fact, none of the additional performers seemed to have any difficulty at all finding their niche within the song. Two young men who squatted and drummed on plastic, five-gallon pails were in perfect sync; a boy and girl, clad in matching sweatsuits, danced a dance that appeared choreographed—one would think they had been practicing it for months. Soon, a mustachioed saxophone player arrived and dove into the melody with righteous passion.

The gathering of spectators became a crowd, and the crowd became a throng. The song had no beginning or end. Born of a few randomly stroked chords, the song grew and swelled until it was something altogether new and wonderful. It was not rock or folk, country or pop. It was the world's biggest jam, and at the same time its most personal ballad.

As for the lyrics, they could be described as nothing less than epic, in the most literal sense. Apollo had not repeated a line or a stanza since he began, and he had begun at the beginning—retelling the tales of the gods, one after another, in perfect pitch and meter. There was nothing so much as a chorus or a refrain, but that did not prevent onlookers from humming along, and even singing some lines. It was as though the song were a part of them, a part of their collective memory that they had forgotten and was now being rediscovered.

Apollo sang of Zeus, Hera, and Semele; of Ariadne and Theseus and the Minotaur; of Aphrodite, Athena and Poseidon, Prometheus and Atlas, Chronos and Eros. He sang of the Olympians, the Titans, and the Primordials. He sang of love and war, trickery, and deceit; he sang of light and darkness, of wit and wisdom. He sang of Dionysus. He sang of himself.

The more he sang, the more he remembered, and the more the people around him remembered. They recalled stories from their youth, tales told at bedtime, and books read in school. Fables and epics written on ancient scrolls came alive in the hearts and minds of a hundred people, and then a thousand. These people went forth from the square with a song in their hearts; they hummed and sang as they spread around the city. The melody, infused with legend, reached the ears of tired mothers looking out apartment windows, of frustrated fathers in their cars, of children who huddled, afraid of the unnatural darkness.

In a quiet part of the Don River, a man stood in a battered and beaten gondola, pole in hand. From across the waters came the faint and mystic melody, crooned by the tongues of those mortals who walked along the river's edge. The song reached his ears, and Charlie the Ferryman took it up, made it his own, and sang it low and loud as he cruised along. He spread it wherever the river flowed, and by the time he reached Chipping Park, a proud, golden sun was beginning to burn a hole through the darkness directly overhead, announcing noontime, announcing warmth, announcing life.

※

Dio woke to the sound of traffic in the street outside. He shifted his body and felt a distinct weight on his left shoulder. Peering out through one squinting eye, he saw that Ari was asleep as well, her body half wrapped around him, her silken hair cascading across his chest. The motel was near the business loop, and the honking horns and revving engines made sleep difficult. He had been so determined not to rest, yet they had both ended up on the hotel bed, which was still neatly made beneath him. They must have finally been overcome by exhaustion.

He was about to close his eyes and allow himself a few more minutes respite from the unkind world, when he stopped—car horns, a myriad of engines, the sounds of business as usual in downtown Toronto.

Dio's eyes snapped open. He turned his head to regard the fully drawn shades of the big window on one wall of the room. Soft, warm light glowed from around its edges, creating an illuminated rectangle next to the door. He could hear footsteps on the walkway outside, people calling out to one another. Keys jingling as someone unlocked their trunk.

"Ari!" he practically shouted, jostling her resting head from his shoulder. "Ari! The sun! The sun is up! There is light!"

Ari snorted and mumbled for a moment, then pushed the hair away from her face and gasped as she looked at the same big window that Dio now scrambled toward, having disentangled himself from her. He yanked down on the flimsy shade and let it zip back to the top, rolling itself up like a flapping cartoon tongue.

"Did we...did they..." Ari struggled to form a thought.

"I don't know!" Dio cut in, anticipating her question. "But *something* must have worked!"

They both could feel the difference in the air. It was not just a matter of the return of light, but an absence of something dark that had intruded on the world so slowly that no one had noticed it until it was too late. No one, that is, except Zeus.

At the thought of his father, Dio snatched up his phone and punched in a number from memory. He waited, phone to his ear, as Ari watched, Finally, he hung up and tried another number. Same results.

"He's probably just trying to get home now," Ari said. "Or he may be looking for you. Who knows?"

Dio nodded absently. He was looking vaguely at

himself in the mirror, searching his features for a reflection of his father.

"You know, no one really knows the rules to this game," he said. "There was never any guarantee that defeating The Darkness in the city would get him out of Hades. And my mother..."

Ari walked over to him and put her hand on his cheek. It was soft. And Dio realized that she smelled like lavender. How could she smell so nice? They had been working around the clock—had she snuck in a shower?

"You can find him, Dio, wherever he is," she said, looking into his eyes with something like faith. "You are his son, you are *of* him, and that means that you can find him."

She slid her hand down to his chest.

"If you wish to, you can find him with this."

Dio thought about Ari and the strands of twine that she used to guide him through the night and lead him to the children and consort of Nyx, those who had led him to the Underworld—to the answers that had allowed not only him, but all the gods, to defeat her.

He realized that there was no need for another strand to follow, not when his own royal blood existed in those two other beings which he had still to find. He needed to know that they were free—Zeus and Semele, mother and father. Unless his family was saved, darkness would continue to loom.

Someone passed by the motel room door, humming

a tune. Dio didn't know the song, but something about it struck a chord in him, uplifting him in a way he had not known possible. He looked to Ari and believed her to be affected by it as well. The voice faded and then returned, pausing outside the door, the melody louder and clearer, sung from a strong throat and with joy and a radiant conviction.

Dio took three long strides toward the door and swung it open. Outside, in the brilliant sunlight stood his half-brother Apollo. He was visibly weary, dirty, and beaming from ear to ear.

"Brother!" Apollo cried, opening his arms wide and stepping into the small room to embrace Dio in a tight and smelly hug. "It is a new day!"

"It sure is," Dio replied, trying in vain to free himself from Apollo's massive arms. "But what are you doing here? How did you find me?"

Apollo released his brother and took a step back into the still open doorway, looking at Dio as though he had asked a ridiculous question. He pointed to the doorknob, where a long piece of twine had been knotted.

Apollo looked at Ari and then Dio, then back at Ari. Sly realization sparked his features.

"Lovely Ari here leaves a good trail, for those who seek the right things," he said. "And for those who know what to look for."

Dio turned his gaze to Ari, who blushed and shrugged, uncharacteristically sheepish.

"You never know when you might need a little help," she said.

Dio could not disagree.

※

"The portal moves, you know," Apollo said. "It was once beneath the Acropolis, once near the dungeons of Nero. Once, I heard it was located somewhere within the Golden Nugget Casino."

They were walking through sun-bright city streets. Most people seemed to have declared the day an official holiday—and rightfully so. Everywhere, on every green space and every park bench, people gathered and talked and laughed. They reveled in the sun, hugged, and conversed. And, Dio could not help but notice, stories and songs of the gods were on every tongue.

"I understand that. I know it could have moved since the other night," Dio said. "But it's all we've got to go on right now. We have to hope."

He knew that Apollo had been the one to finally push back The Darkness. He did not have to ask. When Dio had finally collapsed in exhaustion, the collective and miraculous power of Hestia and Athena, along with Aphrodite's new dog and her #ilovezeus hashtag, had set the scales of good and evil on an absolute balance, and even a small miracle could have tipped the fate of the mortal world in one direction or another. But what Apollo did was no small miracle. He ignited the hearts and minds of thousands with his music; he reinfected the legends and lore of the pantheon back into popular culture, effectively driving Nyx and her dark force back into the nether realms, where she could do little to affect the souls of mortals. He had summoned the sun, willed its emergence from behind Nyx's tar-like veil.

Now, mighty Apollo had sworn to help him find their father—and Dio's birth mother—at all costs. Again, Dio asked for no details, no reason for Apollo's sudden allegiance. Zeus was Apollo's father as well, to be sure, but the two brothers had never cooperated before. He did not concern himself with Apollo's reasons for doing so; he knew he would need Apollo's strength to face whatever lay waiting in the Underworld.

At last, they came to the narrow alleyway where Dio had found Cerberus waiting. It seemed so long ago now, and as Dio entered the alley and regarded the blackened spots on the pavement, where the three-headed dog had slain the Keres, he felt as though he had aged years in just a short amount of time.

The red door was closed, locked tight, and the alleyway looked for all the world like any other back street in any other city in the world.

Apollo tried the knob again, this time shaking the door and straining against the hinges, but to no avail. Dio ran his fingers through his hair; it was greasy and lank, he needed to bathe, and he wondered if and how he would re-enter the Underworld without the help of some ally. He had grown more certain that his father remained imprisoned in Hades' vault, as the day had grown long and there was still no sign of Zeus. Surely, if he had been miraculously freed when Nyx was driven back into the shadows of the netherworld, he would have sought out his sons by any means possible. Now, Dio feared that his father—as well as his mother—may be paying the price at the hands of a vengeful and primordial god.

Apollo leaned back and kicked the door with his heavy combat boot. The sound was deafening, but the attack left not so much as a scratch on the door. He kicked twice more and then was interrupted by an awful and monstrous sound, as though someone were dragging a dumpster behind a semi-truck.

They froze, waiting. The sound came again, louder this time, deep and rending, a guttural shaking of the earth beneath their very feet. When the sound came yet again, it was upon them, though Dio could see nothing at all in the alleyway besides his brother.

Then, there was a flicker of darkness, of black and brown, a shifting of the air and the smell of some dank beast. Apollo was suddenly lifted from his feet, he hovered in the air like a puppeteer's marionette, legs dangling. He looked suddenly wet. Dio smiled.

"What's going on?" Apollo shouted, flailing his arms to no avail. "Help me, Dio! What are you laughing about?"

There was another flicker of motion and a gleam of

one bright, yellow eye. The eye seemed to be smiling, though the growling continued. Apollo's body swung left, then right, before being tossed back to the left, where he landed with a crash in a pile of garbage. Dio burst out in hysterical laughter, for a moment forgetting himself and his task, before he was lapped at by a gigantic and only semi-visible tongue.

"Easy, easy big fella!" Dio said, holding out his hands to repel another tongue bath. "I've got something for you, just calm down."

Dio dug in his jacket pocket and produced a package of salami.

"Is that what I was smelling?" Apollo asked as he extracted himself from the garbage pile. "I thought you just needed a shower."

"You're not smelling so hot yourself there, bud," Dio said as he tossed the salami up into the air, where it disappeared with the sound of snapping jaws. As Cerberus ate, he slowly made himself visible again, the two heads that were not chewing scanning carefully back and forth, wary of mortals. Dio reached up and scratched an ear.

"Hey buddy, I came back," he said. "And no vultures this time. This is Apollo. He's a friend."

Cerberus looked at Apollo and curled a lip on one of his heads but did not attack. Apollo stood as still as a statue.

"Brothers, even." Apollo said, pointing repeatedly at himself and Dio.

Dio suppressed a smile. Apollo had always been more of a cat person.

"Hey Cerb," Dio spoke. "I was hoping to get back inside. I have some unfinished business downstairs."

Cerberus dipped his head and gave Dio a friendly sniff, then he grunted and, with a click, the red door unlocked and swung open.

"Thanks, friend." Dio turned to enter the passageway and Apollo moved to join him but stopped dead in his tracks when Cerberus stepped between them and snarled, saliva showing bright on his long, deadly fangs.

"Hey, hey buddy! He's with me, remember?" Dio said.

But Cerberus shook one of his heads "no" as the other two kept their flashing yellow eyes on Apollo, lest he make a move. Dio felt the vibration of a glowing coin in his pocket and understood that he had not been granted a magical key, but a ticket. Dio looked past the dog at the sun god's pale face and sighed. Apollo, shaken as he was, managed a weak smile.

"Looks like it's a solo mission, bro," he said. "Go on ahead. I'll be waiting up here...well...down the block a bit. You'll do great. I believe in you."

Dio hesitated, then nodded, turning slowly to again face the lush green steps that would lead him down into the Underworld. He couldn't help but think it kind of funny: suddenly, everyone believed in him.

DIO IN THE DARK

AT THE EVENTUAL FOOT OF THE STAIRS, WHERE ANY semblance of material construction ceased and the passageway was a mossy and rocky slope, Dio found that the terrain had not changed, but the atmosphere was far different than on his first visit. The once dead air was charged with rage, storm clouds blew through the grey skies at impossible speeds, black wraiths and the ghosts of terrible birds screamed through the sky and dove at anything that moved—and there were many things that moved.

The ground was covered with creature of all sizes, running or limping or skittering about. Skeletal beings, some great, some small, moved in every direction, panicked, seeking shelter of any type as they were beset by the terrible flapping creatures in the air.

Over and above it all was a tone, or several tones, all seeming to come from some inhuman throat. There was a moan, a groan, a scream, a shriek, one over another, creating an awful and soul-searing sound that filled the expanse of land from bleak horizon to bleak horizon. It drowned out the frantic cries of the pitiful creatures and the crashing of the rapid and rainless storms.

Dio looked about, trying to get his bearings. There was lightning everywhere, but nowhere so much as the distant cliff that was now visible in all of its electric ferocity. He knew that this was where he would find his father. He feared it was also where he would find his mother.

It was difficult crossing the plain. He was beaten down by winds and forced to crawl over the carcasses of fallen creatures as the terrible and screeching birds and ghosts of the air swept over him. He sensed a familiar presence, a scornful trio, and he knew that the Keres roamed above. Once they located him, they would desire nothing more than his blood on their talons.

He felt utterly naked, exposed. How would he ever reach his parents without being torn to ribbons? He was scarcely more than a mortal in this place, alone and in danger. Then a thought came to him. Less a thought, more a sound—a melody. He realized that it was the song that Apollo had been humming and singing at the motel. His brother had continued to harmonize on the song as they travelled to the gate of the Underworld, and now in this chthonic place, Dio had it imprinted in his memory. Somehow, he knew—though he could not explain why—that Apollo was somewhere above, standing under the brilliant sun, singing a song for him.

It was a prayer and a battle cry; a hymn and a suit of armor. Dio began to hum the tune, then he sang aloud, softly at first, words falling to him like rain from the heavens. He sang of them all: of the old ones and the bad ones, the gods who fought and killed and died. Dio found himself singing even of himself, and when he sang of himself, of Dionysus, god of wine, he could not help but begin to sing about fair Ariadne.

His voice grew louder, and he walked more upright. His song repelled the shrieking and screaming devils in the sky; they rasped and squealed and begged him to cease, but they would not—could not—touch him.

With his head high and his chest full of fire and voice, Dio marched across the barren landscape of the Underworld, heading for the blazing cliff where Zeus was imprisoned, being punished, tortured for the failure of Nyx to overtake the world of the mortals.

As he approached the cliff, he saw a figure standing atop it—a pale-faced woman. Something about her was eerily familiar, and distressingly irregular. As Dio got closer, he could see the remnants of a face—mangled with hate and staring venomously toward him with pit-like eyes. Three vultures flew around her, cawing and screeching.

"Mother! Mother! Mother!"

Her feet floated slowly up from the ground. With the chorus of a dark cacophony, the pale-faced woman, and her vultures, were absorbed into the darkness surrounding them.

Voices that screamed and moaned above all else began to separate and form words that spoke directly into Dio's mind, as though it were his own doubts and self-consciousness speaking to him, though he knew in an instant who was speaking to him. Nyx, the goddess manifestation of darkness. She was angry, wrathful, and intent on snuffing out a life. Or as many lives as she could.

You are not worth your father's love. Your mother faded to dust and forgot you. Your followers can never remember your name when they awake with pounding heads and dry tongues. You, Dionysus, are nothing more than the god of hangovers; you are regret, you are what everyone wishes they could undo. I will undo you. Weak child, you are finished.

Dio shook his head to clear his mind. The words tore at his very soul and he wanted to drop to his knees and wail at the wind, to tear at his own flesh and become a wraith. But the song stayed in his soul— Ariadne and Hestia; Athena and Apollo; Aphrodite; even Charon. He was not alone, he was never alone, he was a part of a history that had upheld nations and imaginations for thousands of years. He was a part of a network of inspiration, of love and lust and greed and cautionary tales as well as tales of honor.

He sang again. He sang of Zeus and his lover, Semele, and he pushed the voice of Nyx out of his mind as he neared the cliff, where he could now see the stricken body of his father among the bolts of lightning and the pieces of stones that had broken away from the rock face and skittered down into the valley. In the valley was the golden light, the orb of ash and warmth, a storm within a storm.

Mother.

He reached the orb and sang of an old crone that planted bitter doubt in his mortal mother's mind and whispered dark instructions to his mother's ear. He sang of how his father was tricked into murdering his beloved the very day she told him that she was with child; the story of the baby that Zeus sewed into his thigh—he was singing his own story, the story of Dionysus, the Twice-Born.

The orb glowed bright. Dio raised his eyes to see his father, smiling down on him.

He touched the orb and felt his mother's love course through his body. He was warm and happy, tearful joy streaking his face, even as the malevolent powers of Nyx roiled the air about him and threatened his sanity.

Another voice entered his subconscious and spoke into him. This one was soft, gentle, and earnest.

You have done well, my son. You have defeated her, and she is too weak to pass through the portal. It will be millennia before the mortals forget again, millennia that she must wait now.

"She can never be allowed to do this again," Dio said. "I can destroy her."

I wish it were true, my brave boy, but you must take your father and leave this place. You will be safe. You will lead a happy life again, as you did in the old times. Try not to forget about your mother, for I am always remembering you.

"No," Dio said. "I will not forget you. I can't leave you here, not like this."

As the sky coalesced into an ink-black cloud, absorbing every wraith and bird, every screaming, hateful, bloodlusting thing, Dio crouched and bent over the orb. The sky descended upon him with a crushing weight; it was instant night, filled with razor blades and shards of bone. It tore at his back as he folded his limber body, desperately protecting the glowing light until it was completely wrapped in his being.

The black squall twisted and whipped, blocking Dio from the sight of anything that may have paused long enough in that terror to watch the scene unfold. Zeus remained chained and struggling on the cliff above, though the lightning had ceased, drawn into the energy of the cataclysm that now enveloped both his son and his former, mortal lover.

A thick, black void fell upon them. Heavy. Suffocating. Malevolent.

Dio could feel broken bone and gale wind ripping at his body, knocking him hard to his side. He scrambled back to his knees, steeling his resolve; desperately protecting the orb from the dark storm beyond his body.

Two voices—one drenched in vinegar, the other in honey—fought for dominance in Dio's ears and soul.

God of nothing.
Be brave, my son.
God of nothing.
For we will always love you.
God of nothing!

. . .

As the storm tightened further, creating a black maelstrom of terror at the foot of the cliff, there erupted a cluster of vibrant green beams of light. The beams pierced through the black mass like swords through flesh, and countless awful screams sounded from every corner of the Underworld. The green lights shifted like searchlights, obliterating The Darkness and carving the concentrated evil of Nyx's final attack into tiny fragments that fluttered and drifted away on a wind suddenly filled with the scent of lavender.

Zeus' chains dissolved like sugar in a pot of hot water. He slid down the cliff with the expert skill of a mountain climber, coming to a stop at the place where his son, Dionysus, sat curled in a tight ball, with his forehead touching the earth.

Zeus reached out and touched his son on the shoulder. Dio stirred and slowly straightened up, revealing the thing that he held in his hands. No longer an orb of light and ash, but a flower, purple and vibrant and more beautiful than any other in the world, above or below.

EPILOGUE

Dio sat on a bench by the Don River. The sun, late in arriving, was departing right on time, creating a stunning sunset over the city. Beside him, Ari sat, absently making a cat's cradle with a length of twine between her fingers.

They sat wordlessly, comfortable in the silence, listening to the sound of Charlie the ferryman. He was poling his broken gondola into the gathering mist, barely visible in the fading light. Stars began to poke through the purpling atmosphere. Dio smiled, knowing that, as Charon sang in the twilight, he was piloting a precious passenger—a beautiful flower—from one shore to the next.

GLOSSARY

Aphrodite—Goddess of Love and Beauty. Daughter of Zeus and Dione.

Apollo—God of the Sun, Music, Poetry, and Prophecy. Half-brother of Dionysus. Son of Zeus and Leto.

Ariadne—The daughter of King Minos and Pasiphae. She is best known for helping Theseus face the Minotaur.

Athena—Goddess of Wisdom, Courage and Crafts. Daughter of Zeus and Metis.

Atlas—A titan condemned to hold up the sky/celestial heavens for eternity. (He is commonly misattributed to having to hold up the Earth.)

Cerberus—"The hound of Hades"; three-headed guard dog that blocks the path in and out of the Underworld.

Charon— A ferryman who carries the souls of the

deceased across the River Styx and into the Underworld.

Chronos—The personification of Time.

Daphne—A tree nymph who is turned into a laurel tree in order to escape from Apollo (who was enchanted by Eros).

Dionysus—God of Wine, Ritual Madness, and Agricultural Fertility. Half-brother of Apollo. Son of Zeus and Semele.

Erebus—The primordial deity that represented the personification of darkness; brother and consort to Nyx. Father of the Keres, Hypnos, and Thanatos.

Eros—God of love and sex; often referred to as "Cupid" (his Roman counterpart).

Hades—God of the Underworld, Death, and Riches. Brother to Zeus, son to titans, Cronus and Rhea.

Hera—Goddess of Women, Childbirth, and Marriage. Traditionally married to Zeus. Daughter of titans, Cronus and Rhea.

Hestia—Goddess of Home, Hearth, and Family. Daughter of titans, Cronus and Rhea.

Hypnos—The primordial deity that represented the personification of sleep. Twin brother to Thanatos. Son of Nyx and Erebus.

Ino—A mortal queen, and sister to Semele, who helped raise her nephew, Dionysus. She was deified later in life.

Keres, the —Female death spirits with a gruesome appearance, known for hovering over battlefields in

GLOSSARY

search of dying soldiers. Daughters of Nyx and Erebus.

Minotaur—"Mino's Bull", a mythological monster from Crete; it had the body of a man, and the head of a bull.

Nyx—A primordial deity that preceded the Titans and the Olympians, and was considered the personification of night.

Olympus, Mt.—The highest mountain in Greece; considered the home of the Greek gods.

Poseidon—God of the Sea; Son of titans, Cronus and Rhea.

Primordials, the —Sometimes referred to as the "Protogenoi," these deities were the first to come into existence.

Prometheus—The titan god of fire, credited with creating humanity from clay.

Semele—A princess of Thebes. She was the only mortal to become the parent of a god. She is the sister of Ino.

Sisyphus—The kind of Ephyra, punished for cheating death, and condemned to roll a boulder up a hill for eternity.

Tartarus—The deepest part of the Underworld, which was considered to be a primordial deity in itself.

Theseus—A Greek hero, most famous for slaying the Minotaur, and escaping its labyrinth (with the help of Ariadne).

Titans—The Titans were the Greek gods that ruled

the world before the Olympians. The first 12 titans were considered children of the primordial deities — Uranus (the personification of the sky), and Gaia (the personification of the Earth).

Thanatos—The primordial deity that was the personification of Death. Twin brother to Hypnos. Son of Nyx and Erebus.

Underworld—Sometimes referred to as Hades, the Underworld was where spirits travelled to upon death. It was considered to be made up of many areas.

Zagreus—The underworld god of hunting and rebirth. Son of Hades and Persephone.

Zeus—King of the Gods. God of the Sky, Thunder and Lightning. Brother to Hades. Son of titans, Cronus and Rhea.

ACKNOWLEDGMENTS

There are so many people to thank, I honestly don't know where to start. I'll begin at home —my wonderfully supportive wife, Reem, and our beautiful cat, Nessie (aka. my late-night writing companion).

My editor, Dave Pasquantonio, for all his painstaking efforts! Editing is a hard job in itself. But editing for a dyslexic first time novelist is truly a gigantic effort. Dave remained tremendously encouraging, though I can only imagine there were hours of hunching in front of his screen groaning at the sheer abandon with which I use semi-colons and em-dashes.

My cover designer Casey Gerber, who was able to distill my ramblings of what the cover should represent into a truly beautiful representation of the book.

My proofreaders, launch team, and the well-wishers. And to you my reader, for making it this far!

You are all an amazing bunch of people. Thank you.

ABOUT THE AUTHOR

Rizwan Asad is the award-nominated writer behind the blog, Chocolates & Chai. On Chocolates & Chai he provides delicious recipes in an accessible manner.

Rizwan's short stories have previously been published by Jolly Horror Press and Red Penguin Books. He is based in Toronto, but you can visit him online at: rizwanasad.com.

Dio in the Dark is Rizwan's first novella. If you enjoyed it, please consider leaving a review.

- facebook.com/rizwanasadauthor
- twitter.com/yamisohungry
- instagram.com/yamisohungry

Manufactured by Amazon.ca
Bolton, ON